**FERGUSON
CAREER BIOGRAPHIES**

KATIE COURIC

TV News Broadcaster

James Robert Parish

Ferguson
An imprint of ☑ Facts On File

Katie Couric: TV News Broadcaster

Copyright © 2006 by Facts On File, Inc.

All rights reserved. No part of this book may be reproduced or utilized in any form or by any means, electronic or mechanical, including photocopying, recording, or by any information storage or retrieval systems, without permission in writing from the publisher. For information contact

Ferguson
An imprint of Facts On File, Inc.
132 West 31st Street
New York NY 10001

Library of Congress Cataloging-in-Publication Data

Parish, James Robert.
  Katie Couric : TV news broadcaster / James Robert Parish
      p. cm.
  Includes index.
  ISBN 0-8160-5830-X (hc : alk. paper)
  1. Couric, Katie, 1957–   2. Television personalities—United States—Biography.
I. Title.
  PN1992.4.C68P38 2005
  791.45'092—dc22   2005007915

Ferguson books are available at special discounts when purchased in bulk quantities for businesses, associations, institutions, or sales promotions. Please call our Special Sales Department in New York at (212) 967-8800 or (800) 322-8755.

You can find Ferguson on the World Wide Web at http://www.fergpubco.com

Text design by David Strelecky

Pages 99–112 adapted from Ferguson's *Encyclopedia of Careers and Vocational Guidance, Thirteenth Edition*

Printed in the United States of America

MP JT 10 9 8 7 6 5 4 3 2 1

This book is printed on acid-free paper.

CONTENTS

1 Setting an Industry Record   **1**

2 Born to the Profession   **7**

3 Paying Her Dues   **19**

4 *Today*'s Darling   **33**

5 Rising to the Top   **47**

6 Life Changes   **61**

7 A Mighty Media Force   **75**

Time Line   **93**

How to Become a News Broadcaster	**99**
To Learn More about News Broadcasters	**109**
To Learn More about Katie Couric	**113**
Index	**117**

1
SETTING AN INDUSTRY RECORD

In 2001 Katie Couric finalized a deal with NBC-TV that would pay her $65 million during the next five years. In return, Katie, a veteran TV news journalist, would continue as cohost (with Matt Lauer) of *Today*, the network's popular three-hour morning news show. In addition, the bubbly 44-year-old Katie would participate in other NBC News programming and evening specials. By renewing her NBC assignment for a mammoth $13 million a year, Katie became one of the highest paid TV news personalities in the world. With this salary, Katie now shot ahead of distinguished and famous TV journalists such as Tom Brokaw, Ted Koppel, Peter Jennings, Dan Rather, Diane Sawyer, and Barbara Walters.

When Katie was questioned about her new agreement—the biggest in news broadcasting history—she replied, "If NBC thinks it's fair, I think it's fair." And the broadcast network, which earned an annual profit of well over $250 million in advertising just from *Today*, thought their prized news anchor definitely deserved her whopping new salary. NBC News president Neal Shapiro said of Katie, "The great thing is she has so much talent and range, expertise and interests." Katie, known for both her radiant wholesomeness and her seasoned skills as a hard-nosed journalist/interviewer, says of her career, "I get paid not just to ask questions but to get answers."

Katie has proved repeatedly that she can win interviews with hard-to-reach public figures, particularly in the arenas of world politics. Once she gets an interview, she is unafraid to ask tough questions and pursue real answers from her subjects. According to Jeff Zucker, NBC Entertainment president (and a past executive producer of *Today*), "Whether she's interviewing President Bush or Kermit the Frog, she's brought intelligence, wit, and compassion in a way no one before her had and I think she's become the single most important female journalist in this country." Michael Gartner, the former NBC News president who hired her, says of Katie: "She has what my 99-year-old father calls 'an affidavit face.' You look at her

Katie Couric is known for her pleasant personality and hard-hitting interviewing style. (Photofest)

and believe her. People see something in her they relate to and trust."

Today show audience ratings and popularity polls have confirmed again and again that Katie—who began as an official cohost of the weekday-morning program in April 1991—has the sharp abilities and outgoing personality that appeal to home TV viewers. As to her well-regarded journalistic abilities, Katie says, "My only real concern while I'm being provocative and while I'm challenging an interview subject is that I'm being fair."

Pathfinders

Television journalism and opportunities for women in that field have come a long way in recent years. Katie Couric's huge success in this highly competitive field reflects that. According to Sue Simmons, a TV news anchor on WNBC in Los Angeles, when Simmons began in the field in the mid-1970s, it was typical for a newswoman's career to be finished by the age of 40. She says, "As a woman, you were lucky enough to get a job in front of the camera, and that only occurred if you were young and pretty."

In more recent years the standards for female TV journalists have improved. Dianne Doctor, a TV news director in Los Angeles, noted the positive change in late 2003: "I don't know that age is as much a factor [anymore] as credibility. There's a sense that any person, whether it's a man or a woman that has experience and knowledge, is someone the public will turn to. . . . Now there are more [women in the field—both in front of and behind the camera], so just by sheer numbers, some women will have longer careers."

Over the past decades, several successful female broadcasters proved that success in TV news is not merely a matter of good looks and youth. Broadcasters such as Barbara Walters, Leslie Stahl, Connie Chung, Jessica Savitch, Diane Sawyer, Joan Lunden, and Jane Pauley blazed a trail for other females in the industry. It was because of the career achievements of such women that Katie could build her TV news career in the 1980s and thereafter.

However, Katie Couric's journey to great accomplishment has not been all smooth sailing. It has included many roadblocks, setbacks, and personal tragedies. However, none of these obstacles stopped her determination and drive to succeed in her chosen field.

2

BORN TO THE PROFESSION

Katherine Anne Couric was born on January 7, 1957, in Arlington, Virginia, a suburb across the Potomac River from Washington, D.C. She was the fourth and last child (there were already Emily, Clara, and John) of John and Elinor Couric. John was then an associate editor for United Press International, a major syndicated information service that provides news and feature articles to publications around the globe. In subsequent years he would change professions, becoming a thriving public relations executive in the D.C. area. (After John Couric retired, he taught occasional courses at the University of Maryland.) Besides being a housewife and mother to four youngsters, Elinor found time for volunteer work. In later years she pursued her favorite hobby of arranging flower bouquets, and she worked as a part-time sales clerk at a nearby Lord & Taylor department store.

In mid-1957, when Katie was six months old, the Courics moved to a spacious four-bedroom house in Arlington. The redbrick colonial home boasted a well-manicured front lawn dotted with blooming trees. Obtaining this roomy house was a lifelong dream for the Courics, who had grown up in the Great Depression of the 1930s, when no one's financial future seemed hopeful and most people struggled to survive on a day-to-day basis. This economically uncertain upbringing left its marks on Katie's parents. It caused them to instill conservative spending habits in their children. Even as one of the highest-paid broadcasters in the world, Katie is extremely thrifty in her lifestyle and spending habits.

As the youngest member of the Couric household, little Katie had to compete for attention with her three older siblings. From the start Katie displayed a precocious charm: always smiling, always enthusiastic, and full of funny little statements. Emily recalls of her bright baby sister, "Even when she was an infant, we'd put her in her plastic seat and then all sit around and watch her."

Katie's parents valued education highly. They encouraged their children to do well in their schoolwork and constantly expand their knowledge through outside reading and increasing their vocabulary. This education-comes-first atmosphere had a positive effect on little Katie. By the time she began the first grade at the local

Jamestown Elementary School, she was more advanced academically than her classmates. According to the youngster's first-grade teacher there, "When her parents came for conferences, I couldn't think of anything bad to say. She had the sweetest smile you could imagine and absolutely the best handwriting."

In a household full of high-achieving youngsters, Katie quickly developed her competitive instinct. (It was a trait that would prove especially helpful to her when she entered the highly competitive world of TV journalism.) By the time the lively child was 10 she had found a new way of gaining attention. She would take her sisters' yearbooks and study the names of her siblings' classmates. With this information in mind, she would march up to her sisters' peers whenever she saw them around town and say hello to them by name. This gave young Katie quite a reputation in her neighborhood as a socially outgoing girl. Already known for being well organized and sociable, Katie was elected student body president in her last year of elementary school.

Katie was a fun-loving girl who found great joy and humor in her daily life. As she reflected, "I was a real [class] clown who goofed off a lot." On the home front, Katie was the exception in the generally tidy and orderly household. As Mrs. Couric remembered, "I spent a great deal of time picking up after her. I think she thought things straightened themselves out by magic."

It was a confident and outgoing Katie who entered Arlington's Yorktown High in 1972. Full of energy, she participated in such extracurricular activities as gymnastics, track and field, and cheerleading (following in the footsteps of her sisters). She also wrote for the school paper. In the classroom Katie continued to do well, becoming a member of the National Honor Society. As she recalls, "I was the kid whose essay the teacher would read in front of the class."

Rewarding Volunteer Work

Katie's parents encouraged her to do something sensible with her summer vacations in high school. Thus, Katie volunteered for a position with the day camp of the Columbia Lighthouse for the Blind in Washington, D.C. The teenager found this non-paying position quite rewarding. Often Katie would play the piano for her eight young charges, who responded enthusiastically and sang along to her keyboard performance.

On one pivotal occasion that summer, Katie and her campers visited the National Air and Space Museum in D.C. Once there, one of the children, a youngster named Carolyn, expressed deep fear of stepping onto an escalator. With great understanding for the screaming child, Katie patiently explained to the frightened girl how an escalator actually worked and why it was safe for her to ride. The youngster was convinced by Katie's words and rode the moving stairs. This episode left a strong mark on Katie. Years later, when Katie wrote a piece for *Reader's Digest* magazine, she movingly told how her shared experience with little Carolyn had so powerfully influenced her life and career. According to Katie, "Working my way up through reporting jobs . . . I found that—as in my experience with Carolyn and the escalator—I had developed an ability to put folks at ease and make them feel comfortable during even the most potentially contentious interviews. I acquired this ability by learning to be a patient, sympathetic listener at the Lighthouse camp."

Higher Education

In high school, Katie sometimes focused more attention on her extracurricular activities than on her schoolwork. It caused her usually high grades to occasionally slip a bit. There was also an unfortunate instance when administrators at school found Katie in the girls' restroom smoking a cigarette. While Katie insisted she was merely holding the cigarette for another (unnamed) girl, she was, nevertheless, suspended for a few days. However, this incident was a rare exception in Katie's high school career.

After graduating from Yorktown High, Katie had hoped to attend Smith College in Northampton, Massachusetts, as her two sisters had. Unfortunately, she did not have sufficiently high grades to be accepted there. Instead Katie enrolled at the University of Virginia in Charlottesville. Founded by Thomas Jefferson in 1825, the picturesque campus is located inland over 110 miles southwest of Arlington, a drive of about two-and-a-half hours.

At college, Katie applied herself with great energy in the classroom and with extra activities. She wrote for the campus paper, the *Cavalier Daily*, and became an associate editor of the publication. While she pledged and became a member of the Delta Delta Delta sorority, her circle of friends also included students outside this school social organization. During these college years, Katie's interest in journalism grew and she took several courses in the field.

In the summers Katie interned at local radio stations where she began to develop her interviewing skills. She discovered that one of the most important ingredients of being a good interviewer was learning to really listen to what the other person was saying rather than being distracted by thinking about what one was going to ask the subject next.

With her father's guidance, Katie decided to focus her professional ambitions in the broadcasting field, where, as her father reasoned, TV journalists were much better paid than in the print field. (Katie's career choice was a departure from her siblings' careers. Emily was a high school science teacher who later served on a local board of education and thereafter ran for and was elected to the Virginia State Senate. Clara—nicknamed Kiki—became a landscape architect based in Boston, while brother John became an accountant.)

One of Katie's great role models, in these years and later, was Barbara Walters. Walters had been a host of *Today* (1958–76) and then, in 1976, joined the ABC

One of Katie's great role models is TV news broadcaster Barbara Walters (left). (Time Life Pictures/Getty Images)

network to appear on *ABC Evening News*. On this nightly program, Walters worked as part of a team with Harry Reasoner, thus becoming the first female coanchor of a principal network newscast. Katie would later say, "I have so much affection, admiration and respect for Barbara Walters. You know, she is, I think, the hardest-working woman in television. She is relentless. She is aggressive. I really think she's set the standard for everyone. And when I say she really did pave the way and is a pioneer for women, I'm not just giving her lip service."

Entering a New World

Katie graduated from the University of Virginia in 1979 with honors in American studies. Excited to be entering the workforce, she decided to take an immediate stab at becoming a TV journalist.

Although Katie had few contacts then in the broadcast world, this did not stop her. At the time, the three U.S. TV networks (ABC, CBS, and NBC) all had their headquarters in New York. However, their news divisions each had smaller support offices in the nation's capital. Ambitious, secure, and aggressive, Katie decided to contact the ABC News Washington bureau, where she also had a slight connection to an executive.

Mustering her confidence, Katie arrived at ABC News in Washington, D.C. Using charm and creativity she convinced the security guard on duty to let her talk on the house phone to David Newman, the executive producer of *World News Tonight* (which was based out of the Washington facility). As Katie recalled years later for *Good Housekeeping* magazine, "I said, "Hi, Davey, this is Katie Couric, you don't know me, but my sister Kiki went to Yorktown [high school] with Steve and Eddie, your twin brothers. Do you think I could come up?"

Katie's senior yearbook photo from the University of Virginia, 1979 (University of Virginia)

Upon meeting Katie, Newman was sufficiently impressed with her as an ambitious, dedicated person that he soon hired her for an entry-level post, as a desk assistant. While she had a great many tasks to accomplish in the high-pressure environment, she was thrilled to have made her entry so quickly into the field. She was also awed at mingling with some of the network's key news people, including the fast-rising Sam Donaldson, who was then ABC's chief White House correspondent. Donaldson took an instant liking to the newcomer.

When they met on Katie's first day on the job, Donaldson asked Katie her name. When she told him, the newscaster immediately recalled an old song ("K-K-Katie") and jumped on a nearby desk and began singing its lyrics. Finishing his impromptu performance, the jovial Donaldson invited Katie to join him for an upcoming briefing at the White House. Katie was thrilled that, on her first day at the job, she was to go to the White House.

Katie remained at ABC for less than a year. At that time, George Watson, the bureau chief at ABC News in Washington, D.C., left to join Cable News Network (CNN). This was a new company founded by Georgia-born Ted Turner. CNN began operating as a 24-hour, 7 days a week, all-news operation in 1980. Based in Atlanta, the new network established itself as a premier news organization within a few years, delivering its programming worldwide via satellite. When Turner's outfit hired Watson to join the CNN team and be in charge of the network's Washington bureau, he took several staff members with him. These included both Katie and her coworker, good friend, and apartment mate, Wendy Walker (then a secretary who would eventually move up to becoming a CNN executive producer).

At CNN, Katie was an assignment editor. It was her responsibility to hand out story ideas to reporters and to assign pieces to the news team to be covered for the coming day. Sometimes her duties included doing brief on-air pieces. (Katie recalls, "I wasn't a full-fledged reporter by any stretch. At first, at CNN, the janitor could get on the air. They were often desperate for people to cover events.")

Despite Katie's enthusiasm for her overall job, she was constantly flustered by these on-camera duties. When she was nervous, her voice became high-pitched and screechy, and her hands fluttered. Adding to her problem, the short, fresh-faced Katie looked younger than her 23 years. This led the company's executives—all men at that time—to decide that Katie did not have a seasoned enough look or a sufficiently serious manner to progress very far as an on-air TV personality. This decision was confirmed one day when Reese Schonfeld, CNN's president, phoned his Washington bureau chief. Schonfeld had just seen Katie do an on-camera piece and her voice was so squeaky that he announced angrily, "I never want to see her on the air again."

Katie was crestfallen when she heard the bad news. According to Chris Curle, a CNN coanchor, "I'll never forget how depressed she was that day." Although Katie was discouraged by this turn of events, she was sufficiently grounded to look at her situation sensibly. As she informed *Newsweek* magazine subsequently, "I stunk. I had nobody on my way up saying, 'We're going to make you a star,' and I think that really helped me. It forced me to work."

Determined to prove herself, Katie applied herself even more diligently at CNN, working behind the camera. In 1982, when Chris Curle and her husband, Don Farmer, relocated from D.C. to Atlanta to head up a new CNN show, *Take Two*, they asked Katie to go with them and become the program's producer. Helping her colleagues make this two-hour news/information show come together each day was a big step forward for Katie. It proved that her hard work was paying off.

3
PAYING HER DUES

When Katie Couric moved to Atlanta to work on CNN's *Take Two,* she spent her "free" time with a voice coach who trained the cub TV reporter on how to better project (and lower) her speaking voice. The lessons began to have a positive effect. Meanwhile, Don Farmer and Chris Curle, *Take Two*'s coanchors, were impressed by Katie's skills as producer of their daily show. They went out of their way to give Katie on-the-job career opportunities to expand her experience. Said Curle, "Katie was really a spark plug. She always wanted to do more. As soon as she mastered something, she'd see something else she wanted to do and say, 'I think I can do that. Let me try. I can do that.'" On occasion, they even arranged for Katie to be on air—unofficially—as part of their daily two-hour program. (No one from the network's upper ranks seemed to take notice or complain about her unauthorized appearances.) As time passed, Katie's live performances helped her to improve her skills and confidence as an on-air interviewer and reporter.

Having demonstrated her abilities on the air, Katie later became a permanent on-camera correspondent on *Take Two*. When Farmer and Curle flew to Cuba in 1982 for a three-hour telecast from Havana, they took Katie with them. In typical fashion Katie did a great deal of prep work for this special visit to communist dictator Fidel Castro's island. She even learned some simple Spanish so she could communicate—somewhat falteringly—with local TV workers helping with the live broadcast. Besides charming her Cuban coworkers, Katie got to be in front of the camera for this important news special. Her greatest reward occurred when Reese Schonfeld, CNN's president, later called Katie to compliment her on her contributions to that broadcast.

By 1984 CNN needed extra staff to cover the U.S. presidential election. Katie received a temporary post as an on-air political correspondent for the network. In this capacity Katie did on-camera reports on both the presidential race (between Ronald Reagan and Walter Mondale) as well as interviews and updates on several key run-offs for the U.S. Senate.

After completing this high-profile assignment, Katie hoped that CNN would now offer her a position as a full-time TV reporter. To her great disappointment, the network suggested that she would be better suited to a staff writing assignment. To Katie this seemed a career setback. Puzzling over how to deal with this frustrating turn of events, Katie sought the advice of Don Farmer and Chris Curle who, besides being coworkers, had become Couric's close friends, boosters, and mentors. According to Farmer, "We advised her to leave."

Striking Out on Her Own

Scouting for fresh career opportunities, Katie accepted a position with Miami TV station WTVJ as a full-time, general assignment on-air reporter. She relocated to southern Florida in late 1984 and began her new professional duties, which gave her a lot of on-camera visibility. Working for this NBC-affiliated station, Katie reported twice daily to Miami home viewers on late-breaking news stories. At the time the city was a hotbed of controversial issues, such as immigration, drug trafficking, and repeated crime waves. To keep abreast of local events as they were happening, Katie monitored the Miami police scanner daily, hoping for tips on hot news stories. Determined to prove herself at the station, Katie willingly worked long hours on a daily basis and often spent her weekends toiling at WTVJ. Her special series on child pornography—which she wrote and produced while at WTVJ—earned her industry recognition and awards.

Although Katie had come a long way in a few short years, she still found doing live interviews nerve-wracking. She much preferred those times when she could tape the interview session in advance, because then she could edit any of her flubs. While she was solid in her research and finding of useful contacts to compile the hard facts of a news story, she still had not mastered the art of the graceful on-air interview. Tammi Leader, Katie's producer at WTVJ, told *TV Guide* in 1993 that Couric was "terrible live. She didn't know how the earpiece worked, and she didn't know how to address the camera. She screwed up all the time. She was smart and knew how to put stories together, but her presentation was terrible."

Reflecting back on this demanding period of learning under pressure, Katie recalled that, at the time, she still preferred being a TV reporter to doing news anchoring or live interviews. She reasoned, "I'm not glamorous. I always thought of myself as the workhorse street-reporter type. And besides, my bosses never encouraged me."

By late 1986 Couric had left WTVJ and Miami and returned to Washington, D.C., which also put her closer to her family in Virginia. In Washington she joined the local NBC-TV affiliate, WRC, as a general assignment reporter for the 11:00 P.M. newscast. Her beat was covering such local news topics as municipal corruption, crime, and fires. By now, as she approached age 30, Katie had absorbed a great deal about the broadcast business, but she had much to learn as her responsibilities increased. Moreover, she still had to contend with her less-than-perfect on-air performance when conducting interviews. In addition, she faced a series of roadblocks in the still male-dominated TV news field: (1) she was female, (2) she still looked much younger than her years, and (3) she had not developed a sophisticated professional appearance in respect to her clothing or hairstyle. To compensate for these shortcomings, ambitious Katie did her best always to display a highly confident air in the workplace. She never shied away from expressing her professional opinion—even when, for example, her slant on a news story in progress went against everyone else's viewpoint.

Making Herself Known in the Industry

In 1989, during her third year with WRC, Katie did an especially able job in reporting on a dating service geared to the handicapped. So powerful was her serious presentation that she won both a local Emmy trophy and an Associated Press Award. Executives at NBC News's headquarters in New York City took a hard look at Katie after this story, but they still felt she was not ready for the industry's big leagues.

Bret Marcus, WRC's news director, acknowledged of Katie in the late 1980s: "You can throw anything at her and she can handle it." However, he was aware that Katie's nervousness about doing live interviews was a major career stumbling block. As Katie's contract with WRC was coming up for renewal, Marcus made a suggestion. He advised her that she needed to flesh out her news background by being a full-time anchor in a smaller TV market. In such an atmosphere, he reasoned, she could hone her skills further without being under the scrutiny that major market television (such as WRC) brings. Another option, he volunteered, would be to accept a post with NBC as a deputy Pentagon reporter. This relatively low-profile post would help prepare her for a higher-visibility network position in the future.

Still more focused on being a TV reporter than an anchorperson, Katie pursued the Pentagon job route.

There are at least two versions of how Katie captured this step-up-the-ladder post. According to Fred Francis, NBC's chief Pentagon correspondent, who had been raised in Florida, "I saw her [Couric] doing some police crime stories in Miami several years ago. I asked some of my police sources about what kind of a reporter she was and they said, 'Very aggressive.' " Francis had also been impressed by Katie's more recent live coverage from Dover, Delaware, where she reported on the explosion aboard the USS *Iowa* that killed several service personnel.

In contrast, Tim Russert, NBC Washington bureau chief at the time, remembered, "A lot of people take credit for [Couric]...." He recalled, "I was looking for a general-assignment reporter and I had viewed roughly sixty tapes from all over the country, but I kept glancing up at the monitors and noticing Katie Couric. She was always so competent and unflustered, whether she was covering hard news, soft news, the homeless, or the former mayor of Washington, D.C...." Russert interviewed several dozen candidates before finally offering the position to Katie.

On the Career Rise

In July 1989 Katie began her reporting job at the Pentagon. Eager to succeed in this tough news beat, she went into high gear from the start. A rival reporter at the Pentagon recollected, "She was visible from day one.... She may look sweet and innocent, but she'll steal your lunch." Katie's supervisor, Tim Russert, recalls that Katie displayed a knack for persuading key individuals at the Pentagon to tell her pivotal information. With her wholesome personality that put people at ease, she softened up often tough-to-crack news sources. Some of her contacts were so charmed by Katie that, on occasion, a few of them sent her flowers—which her professional ethics forbade her to accept. Sometimes Pentagon officials would pin information notes to her office door that led to breaking news. She quickly began gaining scoops that made her peers (mostly all males) envious.

In late December 1989, some five months after Katie began covering the Pentagon, the U.S. military invaded Panama hoping to uproot General Manuel Noriega's regime as dictator of that Central American republic. Immediately NBC's Fred Francis was dispatched to Panama City to report on the turmoil there. This left Katie to provide NBC with coverage from the Pentagon. Because of the critical world situation, Couric's live broadcasts came under deep scrutiny from her network superiors based in Manhattan. They were so impressed with Katie's earnestness and freshness on-camera that, scarcely a week after the Panama Invasion, she was asked to anchor the *Saturday Nightly News* in Washington, D.C.

Meeting Prince Charming

When Katie Couric returned to Washington, D.C., to accept her job at WRC, she roomed with her CNN friend, Wendy Walker. It provided Katie with a comfortable home environment on the rare times when she was not working on assignments. With her demanding, nonstop work schedule, Katie found little occasion to handle domestic chores, let alone dating as much as she would like. That all changed in 1988.

Attending a party in the nation's capital, she discovered that most of the men in attendance were attorneys. She did not hide the fact that, in general, she did not think much of members of that profession. One of the other guests at the gathering that night was John Paul Monahan III, known as Jay to his friends. He observed Katie's reaction to meeting several lawyers there. Thus, when the two of them first began to chat, Jay told Katie he was an artist. She was immediately impressed by this handsome painter who displayed such a good sense of humor. When he asked her for a dinner date she agreed. However, she became a bit suspicious of Jay when he confessed later that he was an attorney. (She soon came to overlook this "shortcoming.")

Born in 1954, Jay Monahan grew up in Manhasset, New York. He graduated from Washington and Lee University in Lexington, Virginia. While there he earned high grades and played lacrosse and football. Following graduation he enrolled at Georgetown University Law School in Washington, D.C. During his three years there he became editor of the *Georgetown Law Journal*, a very prestigious honor. After graduating with distinction, he served as a law clerk for a U.S. District Court judge. By the time Jay met Katie, he was an attorney associated with the

D.C. law firm of Williams and Connolly, where he practiced trial and appellate criminal and civil law.

Jay's chief hobby was a passionate interest in the U.S. Civil War, and he had already acquired an impressive collection of Civil War relics. Often, in his spare time, he participated in the elaborate battle reenactments staged on sites of past Civil War clashes. Initially, Katie had no interest in her boyfriend's avocation. However, as time passed, she grew to respect his hobby in which he had invested so much time, energy, scholarship, and money.

Following nearly a year's courtship, Jay visited the Courics in Virginia and asked Katie's parents for permission to wed their daughter. They happily gave their consent. When the groom-to-be inquired if there was anything he should know about his future wife, Mr. Couric responded, "She can be a pouter."

Katie and Jay wed in 1989. Because of her Pentagon assignment, Katie had little time for their honeymoon. In fact, on the celebratory trip Katie brought along—to study—a thick military manual detailing various armed forces vessels and equipment. The newlyweds set up house in a one-bedroom apartment in downtown Washington.

The couple experienced an initial period of adjustment as the well-ordered Jay learned to cope with Katie's more laid back domestic habits. Nevertheless, the efficient

Paying Her Dues • 29

Katie and her husband, Jay Monahan, in 1995 (Time Life Pictures/Getty Images)

attorney was constantly amazed by his wife's ability to accomplish so much—often at the same time. He described, "She'll be lying on the couch, giving attention to our Persian cat, Frank, talking on the phone, watching the news on TV, reading *Newsweek* and *Time* and resting all at once." Soon finding their D.C. digs too cramped—especially for Jay's ever-growing Civil War collection—the couple purchased a house in Virginia. There in a rural stretch of the Shenandoah Valley they resided on weekends in their sprawling, 200-year-old farmhouse.

Leaping Ahead

In spring 1990 Katie Couric's long years of apprenticeship in the TV news field finally paid off. NBC executives offered her a position as the national correspondent for their *Today* program. She accepted the promotion, which allowed her to remain based in Washington with Jay. However, her new routine was soon shattered. When U.S. forces were dispatched to the Persian Gulf in early August 1990 in reaction to Iraq's invasion of Kuwait days earlier, Katie was reassigned back to the Pentagon watch to report on the brewing Persian Gulf War for *Today*.

Having so many inside sources from her days as deputy Pentagon reporter, Katie had solid connections to obtain the latest news on military operations in the Middle East. To keep abreast of breaking information, Katie had to arrive at the Pentagon by 5:30 A.M. so that she could report the latest on the *Today* show when it began its daily broadcast at 7:00 A.M. Because Katie was reporting on such key current events, she had high visibility on the program and became increasingly well known to the show's large audience.

At one point during the Gulf War, Katie was dispatched to Saudi Arabia. It was her debut overseas assignment. There her task was to report on how locals were coping with the chaotic events confronting their country. While abroad, Katie also talked with U.S. troops stationed in the desert war zone. She quickly came to appreciate how war affected American soldiers who were risking their lives in service of their country.

Katie was the first TV reporter to interview U.S. General H. Norman Schwarzkopf, commander of the Allied forces against Iraq, after the Gulf War ended on February 28, 1991. This broadcast gave Katie a high standing in the broadcast industry and deeply impressed home viewers.

4

TODAY'S DARLING

The *Today* show was the brainchild of Sylvester "Pat" Weaver, a Madison Avenue advertising executive who joined the NBC network in 1949 as its vice president in charge of television. Weaver was responsible for many innovations in the early days of television, including the pioneering Saturday night comedy/variety program, *Your Show of Shows*. Weaver also created the late-night talk show format (*Tonight*), the globetrotting cultural news magazine (*Wide, Wide World*), and the women's magazine of the airwaves (*Home*). All of these formats are still vital parts of television programming today.

It was Pat Weaver who also promoted *Today*, network TV's debut early-morning program, which premiered on NBC on January 14, 1952. Weaver's vision for this show was that few home viewers would have the time or interest to watch the entire two-hour daily program as they dressed, breakfasted, and went off to work or school. However, under his direction, the show's design included a news summary every half hour, with short interludes between highlighting weather, sports, features, and interviews.

Waking Up to *Today*

The *Today* show initially aired from midtown Manhattan on the ground floor of the RCA Exhibition Hall. Boasting a large plate-glass window, the studio's setup allowed passersby on the street to witness the program in progress and to be captured on screen as cameras regularly panned over the crowd. The show really gained in popularity in 1953 when J. Fred Muggs, an antic-prone chimpanzee, joined the show. The animal remained with *Today* for four years.

Over the next several years, there was a frequent changeover of staff at *Today*, which was hosted by a male broadcaster. In the early years of the program there was also the "*Today* Girl," a featured position that, over the years, went to various actresses, singers, and beauty contest winners. When host Dave Garroway departed *Today* in 1961, he was succeeded by veteran newsman John Chancellor who, in turn, was replaced the following year by the more light-hearted Hugh Downs. During Downs's reign, *Today* often went on location around the United

States to enhance audience ratings. It was in this period that Barbara Walters, hired as a *Today* staff writer in 1961, began her frequent on-air appearances. By the time Walters departed the program in the mid-1970s, she had become cohost of the enduring morning fare.

After Hugh Downs left the *Today* show in 1971, several other replacements took over the *Today* top spot before Tom Brokaw, an experienced newsman, assumed the lead on-air position. When Barbara Walters vacated the NBC program, she was replaced by Jane Pauley, a young TV news professional. The third key member of the new regulars was good-humored Willard Scott, who joined the show in 1980 to handle weather and feature reports. As 1981 ended, Brokaw was reassigned to coanchor NBC's evening newscast. He was replaced by African-American broadcaster Bryant Gumbel (a past NBC sportscaster) and Chris Wallace (NBC News correspondent). Within a year Wallace had moved on, and the new "permanent" *Today* team consisted of Gumbel, Pauley, and Scott. The effective trio continued to lead *Today* to victory against its closest competitors, ABC's *Good Morning America*.

In February 1989, an annoyed Bryant Gumbel wrote a memo to upper NBC management that was leaked to the press. In unflattering terms, the communication sharply criticized all of his *Today* coplayers, except for Jane Pauley. Although Gumbel later apologized on-air for his misstep, this public relations disaster caused a good number of TV viewers to decide against further welcoming the once-seemingly friendly *Today* family into their home. As NBC discovered, early morning live TV fare had special audience requirements. In those hours of air time home viewers were at their most informal as they dressed and prepared for the day. At that time of the day, viewers wanted to watch agreeable and hospitable on-air personalities to set the right mood for the hours ahead.

In this same troubled year for *Today*, Dick Ebersol, an NBC Sports executive, was placed in charge of *Today.* One of his first moves was to bring Deborah Norville, host of *NBC News at Sunrise*, aboard to read the show's news. To many observers, this seemed to be a move to oust the older, less glamorous Jane Pauley. By that fall, Norville had joined Gumbel and Pauley in the show's opening lineup on the sound stage couch. People's fear of the much-admired Jane being pushed aside by this newcomer seemed to be a fast-approaching reality. Not too long thereafter, Pauley announced she was leaving *Today* to take on other NBC News chores.

With Gumbel, Norville, and Scott now the key figures on *Today,* the program's ratings slipped badly. In February 1991 Deborah Norville went on maternity leave. It was announced that her temporary replacement would be Katie Couric, who was already a *Today* correspondent and,

Three generations of Today *show hosts: (from left) Barbara Walters, Katie Couric, and Jane Pauley* (Photofest)

thus, familiar to the show's nationwide fan base. Weeks later, when Norville stated she was not returning to *Today*, NBC quickly decided that Katie should become *Today*'s new official cohost. Katie began her full-time assignment on Thursday, April 4, 1991. That first day, she was introduced to home viewers by a smiling Bryant Gumbel who announced, "Katie is now a permanent fixture here . . . a member of our family . . . an especially welcome one."

Reporting on TV's fresh-faced new morning personality, who wore a rather short hairstyle compared to other current female newscasters, Walter Goodman of the *New*

York Times decided, "She has a comfortable, easy-to-live-with look, pretty without knocking you off the chair. She's the kind of person you'd want to sit next to at a dinner party." Marvin Kitman (*TV Guide*) judged of the newcomer, "She is enormously engaging on air, especially with teammates. . . . And the beauty of it is that she is actually smart as well as appealing. She is never an embarrassment on the news show."

Finding Her Way on *Today*

As cohosts of *Today*, Katie and Bryant kept the two-hour daily program moving along from segment to segment and feature to feature. A trademark of *Today* had become having the coanchors perform their chores from swivel chairs in a conversation area of the ground-level studio 1A. It was in this area of the sound stage that the guests often joined the cohosts for chats. But the two hours in front of the camera was not the sum of the anchors' daily work. It required a good deal of research (some of which was provided by support staff) and preparation by Katie, Bryant, and *Today*'s other on-camera personalities.

Part of Katie's agreement with NBC News management was that she would be given the same opportunities as Bryant to conduct serious interviews and ask hard questions. (In bygone years, for example, when

Barbara Walters was cohost of *Today,* she was never allowed to initiate questions to a major guest. She had to wait until coanchor Tom Brokaw had asked the first tough questions.)

Initially Katie found her *Today* chores daunting. In her new post she had to combine the proper degree of jauntiness with seriousness as she chatted on-air with the other *Today* regulars, daily guests, and participated in lighthearted fashion and food features. According to Katie, "It was all very new for me and tough at first and I would get very uptight."

Katie and Today *cohost Bryant Gumbel* (Photofest)

Because she had to work in such close harmony with Bryant Gumbel, Katie was no longer a solo act in her on-air time. For example, since Bryant was noted for being such a sharp dresser, Katie had to give even more consideration to her wardrobe, which was usually more functional than fashionable. Then too, since Gumbel had been a cohost regular for several years, newcomer Katie, who had a much bubblier, friendlier on-air personality than her colleague, had to tone down her natural exuberance during her apprenticeship period. Inwardly, she found it somewhat frustrating to have to take her cues in broadcast behavior from Gumbel. However, it was too early in her tenure at *Today* to rock the show's boat.

Improving the Ratings

TV network revenue is based on advertising dollars spent to promote products during shows. The amount a network can charge for advertising during a particular program revolves around the popularity of that program as registered by market share, home viewer ratings, and so forth. NBC executives were pleased to discover that, in comparison to the 3.8 Nielsen ratings that *Today* had during the final week of Deborah Norville's tenure, at the end of Katie's debut week, the Nielsen ratings had jumped to 4.3. This sudden rise helped to close the gap that had existed between *Today* and the then higher-rated *Good Morning America* on ABC-TV. People at *Today* credited Katie's sense of humor and professionalism as major reasons for the ratings shift. A veteran of the morning program informed *Time* magazine, "Katie is friendly, outgoing, news credible. People here are relieved."

The *Today* home viewing ratings continued to climb as Katie performed interviews with the likes of Jordan's King Hussein. Network executives agreed that it was the addition of perky, cute Katie—who could ask those tough questions—that had dramatically boosted the show in the public's esteem. This success led an NBC executive to tell *Time* magazine, "Everybody knew we had seen the future and it was Katie."

As Katie gained more confidence in her expanded on-air work, she took stock of her new industry status and her growing amount of fan mail from viewers. These letters confirmed to her (and to the show's producers) that what appealed most to people about Katie was her naturalness, her sensible, unadorned approach to life, and her knack at cutting to the heart of the matter. Audiences especially appreciated Katie's ability to poke fun at her personal foibles or occasional klutziness in participating in the often-offbeat features on the program. On one such occasion, at an amused Bryant Gumbel's prompting, she forced herself to sample headcheese [i.e., luncheon meat made of the edible parts of the head of a pig or calf]. She won over TV watchers' loyalty as she bravely took a bite of the supposed delicacy that she had just spread on a cracker and then—while making a few faces—had gulped it down.

Such lighthearted, on-air episodes endeared Katie to the public. As she analyzed for the *New York Times* in April 1992, "I think people see me as someone they could have gone to high school with, or someone who works at the desk next to them. I'm ridiculously normal." Of her more serious *Today* chores—doing hard-hitting interviews with major figures on the worldwide news scene—she said to Bruce Weber of the *New York Times*: "People get a sense that I really enjoy talking to who I'm talking to, that I don't see it as a duty, that I see it as a pleasure. I think I have the ability to laugh at myself, which perhaps people find appealing. And I don't think I'm better than other people. I don't have an air of superiority. If anything, I think I'm a bit of a reverse snob. I don't like snobby people myself."

In the passing weeks Couric's self-assurance at *Today* increased. Dissecting the key ingredients of her new position, Katie analyzed, "I think there's much more that goes into anchoring the *Today* show—not just the personality. I feel that I'm using a lot of the skills that I honed as a reporter."

The Pressures of Success

Part of the allure of the high-visibility, much-coveted *Today* assignment was a tremendous increase in salary: Katie's income jumped up to $500,000 a year plus company perks. On the downside, it meant Katie had to be based in Manhattan for her demanding daily tasks. As a temporary measure, Katie decided to rent a New York City apartment while Jay remained at his D.C. job. On weekends and whenever possible he would shuttle to Katie's Manhattan place, or she to Jay's place in McLean, Virginia (a suburb outside of Washington, D.C.), or reunite at their peaceful Virginia farm. It was an exhausting and frustrating situation—with very complicated time schedules that often changed at a moment's notice—that left neither person satisfied. However, the couple agreed that this major career opportunity was far too good for Katie to pass up.

One piece of information which Jay and Katie had kept private in early 1991, when the *Today* show coanchor offer had come onto the horizon, was the fact that Katie was pregnant. When Katie began her new full-time TV broadcasting post in April, she did not yet inform anyone on the *Today* staff of her impending motherhood. She did not want her pregnancy to detract from people's perceptions of how she handled her demanding new chores. In succeeding weeks, as she became accustomed to her extensive responsibilities, she began experiencing morning sickness, which she could not always hide from the program's cast and crew. At this point she informed network officials of her condition so they could plan ahead when she needed to take a maternity leave. By that point NBC officials were so pleased with Katie's impact on *Today* that they readily agreed to schedule substitutes to handle her chores during her time away.

In August 1991, at age 34, Katie gave birth to a baby girl whom she and Jay named Elinor Tully Monahan. The proud parents called their daughter Ellie for short.

After two months away from *Today,* Katie returned to her on-air cohosting duties, having hired a nanny to care for her baby at the Manhattan apartment. Still commuting back and forth, Katie and Jay juggled schedules to be together and to spend time with their newborn. Sometimes Jay took on a legal case in the New York City area, which allowed him to stay full time for that period at Katie's Manhattan apartment. With both of them experiencing a draining daily work routine, neither had time for much socializing—except for business. They counted on old friends to provide their inner circle of entertainment and support. Said down-to-earth Katie, who refused to dramatically expand her lifestyle now that she was an extremely well-paid national celebrity, "My social circle

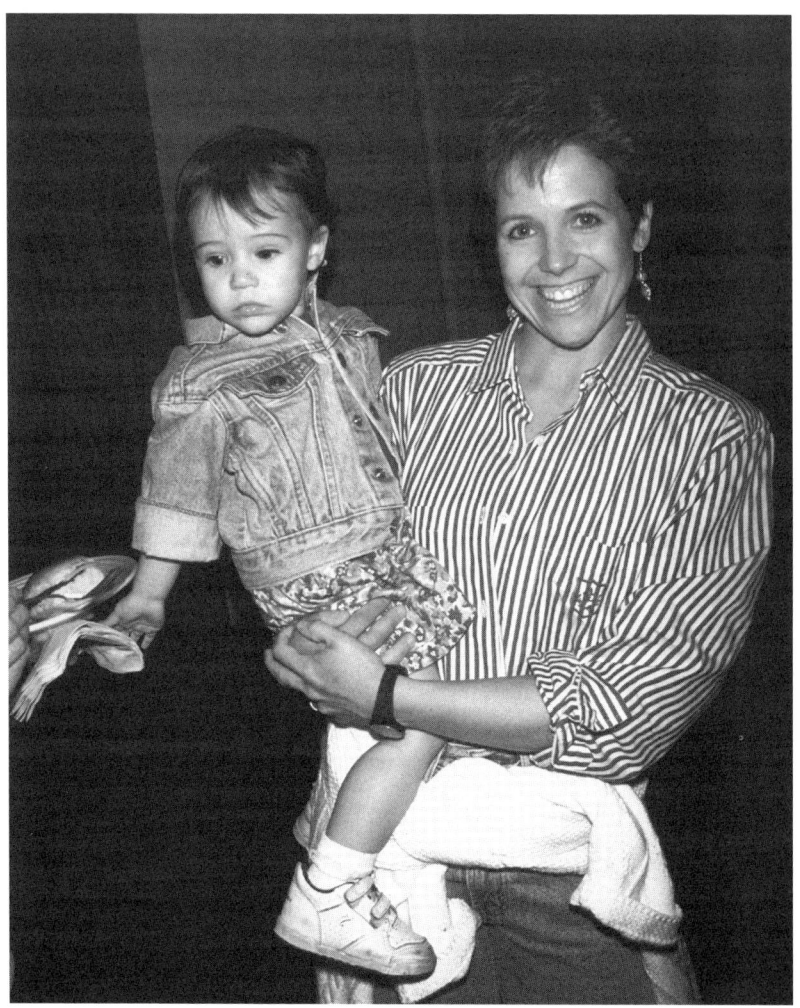

Katie and her daughter Ellie in 1993 (Time Life Pictures/ Getty Images)

hasn't changed. The idea of dumping my friends for fancier friends is sooo gross!"

Back on *Today*, Katie quickly discovered how much her show teammates and American TV viewers had taken her to heart. On her first day back in front of the cameras after her maternity leave, the program scheduled a montage of photos of the new mother and infant so the home audience could share in Katie's joy.

5

RISING TO THE TOP

As Katie Couric settled comfortably into her *Today* show chores and favorable word-of-mouth increased among early morning TV watchers, the program's ratings soared above *Good Morning America* and third-place *CBS Morning News*. In 1992, after Katie had been with the program for a year, she was awarded a new five-year contract. It paid the news broadcaster an impressive annual salary of over $1 million. Explaining Katie's mounting success in her high-profile new post, *TV Guide* senior writer Mary Murphy pointed out that Katie was "probably the first woman on network television in a serious job not to take herself so seriously." The likeability quotient, long a Couric trademark, was paying great dividends for Katie.

To bring back a flavor of the *Today* program from the 1950s, the 1990s version returned to using a "storefront" TV studio overlooking Rockefeller Plaza. In June 1994 the show moved from 30 Rockefeller Plaza, its long-time home, to a new base of operations at the corner of West 49th Street and Rockefeller Plaza. With its huge, three-story high plate-glass (bullet-proof) window in place, passersby could now observe Bryant Gumbel, Katie Couric, Willard Scott, and the other regulars during the live broadcast, which in the later 1990s expanded to a three-hour format. In turn, Bryant, Katie, and the other show staples sometimes ventured out into the Manhattan streets to chat with onlookers.

Now and again, in the course of her job, Katie traveled further than the streets of Manhattan. For the 1992 Summer Olympics, she flew to Barcelona, Spain, where she spent a month covering the games. Each day a bright and animated Katie—who had never been the highly-devoted sports enthusiast that coanchor Bryant Gumbel was—reported on the upcoming events, participants, and appealing sidelights to the colorful proceedings.

A Presidential Interview

That fall Katie flew to Washington to tour the White House with First Lady Barbara Bush. During the live telecast on October 13, Katie and the equally warmhearted first lady proceeded from room to room of the stately quarters, pausing to chat about historical events that had occurred here and there in the famous building. Responding to

Couric's openness on-camera, Mrs. Bush related humorous anecdotes that occurred in the years that she and her husband occupied the White House. As President George Bush was then in the final rounds of his campaign to win the November presidential election, Katie questioned the first lady about his reelection efforts. At this point the president, surrounded by Secret Service agents and accompanied by his dog Ranger, entered the room.

If President Bush thought he could merely exchange pleasantries with pretty Katie and then quickly depart, he had sorely underestimated the enterprising newscaster. Seizing a golden opportunity, Katie—apparently unscripted—launched into a series of tough questions for the president. She asked him about the then much-publicized scandal surrounding the Iran Contra Affair. (At the time, the U.S. Congress was holding hearings to investigate America's purported joint activities with Iran that including shipping heavy-duty weapons to rebel forces in Nicaragua.)

For 19 minutes a determined Katie grilled the surprised President on various hot topics. Whenever he responded with soft answers, she effectively pressed ahead with more direct questions. Trying to put a good spin on the discomforting situation, Bush repeatedly insisted to his petite inquisitor that he was just passing through the White House room and really had to be on his way. However, Katie used all her charm and reporter's skills to keep her subject from bolting. At one point, she quipped to the apparently frazzled President Bush, "Aren't I great? I'm one of those less-contentious reporters who can persuade you to stick around and talk with me because I'm so easy." To which Bush replied, "Easy? I don't want to get in a fight with you." During this amazing impromptu news conference, *Today*'s producer Jeff Zucker, in an off-camera area, stood in amazement and glee as the spirited coanchor held her ground admirably.

Katie's milestone interview with Bush increased her already strong credibility within the TV broadcast industry and with the public. For many in America, Katie's performance under fire showed them just how professional and persistent a journalist she was. As Geraldo Rivera, one of American TV's most aggressive and outspoken news reporters, observed, "Katie is deceptive as a journalist. . . . She is tough as nails."

Refining Her Image

Ever since Katie Couric first came into prominence as a TV newscaster, she had been described by the media as "perky" and "cute." While she indeed possessed both these qualities, she felt they detracted from her abilities as a seasoned and competitive journalist. Thus, in 1993 *Entertainment Weekly* gave Katie a new label: "cool." The magazine reasoned, "How better to describe someone who puts up with Bryant Gumbel's ego and Willard Scott's antics at 7 A.M. five days a week and made the show worth watching again?"

Always the modest diplomat, Katie accepted the compliment in a roundabout fashion: "Cool is something you are when you don't try to be it. . . . if people think you are when you don't try, that's cool." When asked to describe someone she thought was really cool, Katie immediately named Hillary Rodham Clinton whom she had recently interviewed on-air. The *Today* cohost, who had a strong liberal political viewpoint, said of the United States' new first lady, "She's competent and not afraid to be, and incredibly disciplined. She seems like a nice woman, and I guess that's cool."

Katie's demanding *Today* chores kept her on the go daily from 4:30 or 5:00 A.M. till long after dinner when she finished reading staff notes in preparation for the next morning's proceedings. Nevertheless, she found time to make a variety of other television appearances. She did a guest spot as herself on a May 1992 episode of the TV sitcom *Murphy Brown* and had a brief cameo on an April 1993 installment of the TV comedy series *Cheers*. Besides hosting—and often engineering the creation of—informational news specials (such as one about the problems of adolescent girls), Katie was the master of ceremonies of such small-screen offerings as *Legend to Legend Night: A Celebrity Cavalcade* that aired in December 1993.

Besides contributing pieces to *Dateline*, NBC's evening news magazine (where she became a contributing anchor in 1994), Katie was asked by NBC News executives to cohost with Tom Brokaw a new evening news magazine show, *Now with Tom Brokaw and Katie Couric*. Launched on August 18, 1993, this hour-long show, produced by *Today*'s Jeff Zucker, had the usual mix of news stories on pop culture and celebrity interviews.

Despite the best efforts of the seasoned *Now* team, the show was unable to distinguish itself in a TV marketplace stuffed with similarly formatted primetime news/information fare (e.g., the award-winning *60 Minutes*). By early September 1994, *Now* aired for the last time. Thereafter, its time slot and some of its staff were blended into the NBC network's existing evening news magazine, *Dateline*.

A New Lifestyle

After three years of dividing their time between different cities, Katie and Jay established a new domestic setup. He left his Washington, D.C., practice and became associated with the New York office of the law firm of Hunton and Williams. While it may have seemed to outsiders that Katie's success had greatly overshadowed Jay's work achievements, those who knew the couple well insisted that Jay was very pleased—and not at all envious—of Katie's great media popularity.

Now that the couple could finally live together on a full-time basis, they moved from her small duplex apartment to a much bigger place: a four-bedroom apartment overlooking Central Park. There they could share time with fast-growing Ellie, entertain their circle of friends, and relax from their daily work grind. Katie was excited about the new home, saying, "Because I've been a television correspondent for the past fifteen years, I've moved around a great deal. As a result, I've never had a place that was truly done before." She took great joy in furnishing their new home, but, as always, her lifelong thriftiness came through and she found it hard to splurge on extravagant furnishings, even though the couple could well afford to do so.

However, the excitement of a new residence did not reduce the burdens of Katie's high-visibility job. One of the most stressful aspects of the position was the constant race to grab currently famous people for on-air interviews that could boost the show's ratings. The problem was there were only so many celebrities that were of interest to TV audiences. As a result, there was immense competition between rival shows and networks to land exclusive interviews with these newsmakers. Thus, Katie was constantly going against her rivals, including such other skilled female TV news interviewers as Jane Pauley (NBC's *Dateline*), Barbara Walters (ABC's *20/20*), Diane Sawyer (ABC's *Primetime*), Connie Chung (CBS's *Eye to Eye*), and Leslie Stahl (CBS's *60 Minutes*), to get the best interview.

In these ongoing contests with her peers Katie proved to be tenacious, creative, and often successful in wooing an impressive number of key personalities to talk with her on *Today*. Usually, *Today*'s producers and support staff would make the initial contacts with potential V.I.P. guests to book them for the program. If these efforts failed to produce results in time to meet programming deadlines, Katie would step in. More often than not her persuasiveness and the respected position she held within the broadcast community would win over subjects hesitant to appear on *Today*.

Being so highly visible to so many TV viewers, Katie was constantly sought by the media to give interviews revealing the "real" Katie. For an August 1993 *People* article, Karen Schneider provided details on Katie. The writer quoted Katie's past colleague, Chris Curle, then an anchor at an Atlanta TV station, as saying, "With Katie, what you see is what you get." According to Schneider this meant, "A quirky chaotic kind of Everywoman charm affirmed by everyone she touches. . . . Anyone who has crossed Couric's professional path—George Bush, for instance—

knows better than to mistake an impulsive demeanor for an airhead mind."

In lighthearted contrast, the *People* writer learned from Katie's nanny, Nancy Poznek, that "Katie's so messy. Once I let her borrow my black coat, and the next day I took it out and it had chicken bones in the pockets." For this national magazine profile, Jay Monahan recalled the time when the family made their complicated transfer to their new Manhattan address. He acknowledged, "She's no help, because she's too sentimental. I'll ask her to go through her papers to throw things away, but she'll find an old letter from a friend, and the next thing you know she's on the phone for three hours."

The public was also intrigued to learn more about the working relationship between Bryant Gumbel and Katie on *Today*. Everyone agreed that Katie lightened the mood of the show, and that her sprightliness was an effective contrast to the often stern Gumbel. For the sake of the audience, Katie and Bryant created an on-air atmosphere of professionalism and friendliness. It was not until the April 12, 1997, issue of *George* magazine that Katie publicly revealed some of her true feelings about her, by then, ex-cohost. She was quoted in the article as saying, "We were never really that close. There was a lot of creative tension. Well, there was tension. I don't know how creative it was."

Such magazine and newspaper pieces also reflected the tug-of-war of priorities that most working women were experiencing in the 1990s: how to properly balance job duties with domestic responsibilities to loved ones. Katie candidly acknowledged that she was torn between her heavy-duty *Today* chores and finding sufficient time to spend with Ellie. There were occasions, she admitted, when little Ellie would awaken during the night and not even the nanny could calm her. At such moments, the

Because of the high level of respect Katie has earned for her interviewing skills, she has been chosen to meet with many world leaders. Here she is conducting an interview with President Bill Clinton. (Associated Press, The White House)

little girl wanted and needed her mother. The next morning, Katie would arrive to her early makeup call at *Today* in a worn-out state. On such occasions she dispelled her tiredness with cups of studio coffee and counted on the adrenalin rush of going on-air to perk her up.

Adding New Responsibilities

In 1994 major new stories included the attack initiated by Olympic ice skater Tonya Harding against her rival Nancy Kerrigan and the murder of Nicole Brown Simpson and her acquaintance Ronald Goldman, leading to famous sports figure O. J. Simpson, Nicole's ex-husband, being named as the chief suspect. As these and other key current events occurred, the *Today* staff competed in interviewing the chief players.

In 1995 Bryant Gumbel's latest multi-year contract with *Today* was soon due to expire. At the peak of his form, the veteran TV anchorman/host was in high demand. Rival shows and networks sought to lure Gumbel away from the NBC News show where he had worked since 1982. To keep him aboard *Today,* NBC provided Gumbel with another three-year pact, which significantly improved upon his prior $7 million deal. Katie watched these negotiations from the sidelines and wondered if one day she would be in the same enviable position as her cohost.

Further into 1995 Katie had news of her own to share with the extensive home audience. For weeks the viewing public had noted that the usually trim Couric was gaining weight. To answer fans' curiosity, one day on *Today* good-natured Al Roker, who handled the weather and feature reports, came on-camera pushing a baby carriage. With that Katie joked on-air: "I know people think I need to lay off the jelly doughnuts because they haven't seen my waist in weeks." She then admitted that she was expecting another baby.

In October 1995, when the jury in Los Angeles handed down a Not Guilty verdict in the O. J. Simpson double murder trial, it was arranged that Bryant Gumbel (with Katie and Tom Brokaw as part of the team) would question the defendant in his first network TV interview since the trial got underway. Having set up the session, Simpson's legal advisers threw a sudden roadblock into the interview: The lawyers said that because Gumbel had been a longtime friend of Simpson and had often publicly proclaimed his pal's innocence in the double homicide case, it would be improper for Bryant to conduct the upcoming interview with O. J. When NBC officials agreed, it was decided that Matt Lauer, who had joined *Today*'s News Desk in 1994, should take over the Q&A session along with Couric and Brokaw.

This turn of events greatly annoyed Gumbel. He stayed away from the TV studio for a week. Ironically, before long, O. J.'s legal staff found themselves facing a civil suit filed against Simpson by the families of Nicole Brown and Ronald Goldman. As a result, Simpson's legal team decided that he should not participate in any media sessions at this critical juncture. By the time this latest change of plans was announced, Katie and the others were already in L.A. preparing for the big meeting that was not to be. Meanwhile, still smarting over the situation, Bryant announced that although he had another year to go on his (recently-signed) NBC News deal, he planned to leave *Today* thereafter.

On January 5, 1996, Katie gave birth to a baby girl. The Monohans named their new daughter Caroline Couric Monahan. Katie took a two-month maternity leave. When she returned to *Today* in early March, Bryant Gumbel was away and Matt Lauer was substituting as coanchor.

6

LIFE CHANGES

As Katie Couric, now the mother of two young girls, got back into the full swing of her TV journalism career, her image continued to come under public scrutiny. Specifically, there was the matter of her choice of wardrobe. Katie admitted to *Women's Wear Daily*, "Even though I have the best of intentions, I never pick out what I'm going to wear the night before. I'm usually just too tired or I'm studying for the show. So I try to grab what's clean, or something that I think will look OK. That can be a pain. I've worn navy stockings that should have been black on several occasions. I do pretty much get dressed in the dark."

Intent on viewers regarding her as a serious news journalist rather than merely a fashion figure, she confessed that her wardrobe, accessories, and makeup were all geared to having the TV audience pay full attention to what she was saying. As such, Katie gravitated to a classic, tailored wardrobe. "But," added the nearly 40-year-old career woman, wife, and mother: "I try to make them a little interesting, too. I think that if I've become not more fashion-forward, at least I've become more fashion-present. I like to stay in touch with what people are wearing and what's in style. I would like to think I've become more sophisticated as I've aged."

A Challenging Life

By the time that Katie flew to Atlanta to cover the 1996 Summer Olympics she had a second nanny in place in her household, one who could devote herself to the needs of Carrie. This new setup allowed Katie the luxury of sleeping through the night, so that when she arose around 5:00 A.M. to dress for that day's show she would be rested. Although, as a mother, Katie felt guilty at passing on this night watch to another, she was, at least, pleased that her work schedule allowed her to be home by mid-afternoon. As such, she could spend quality time with both children and have dinner with Jay and them.

In the midst of the Atlanta Olympics, tragedy struck. On July 27, a pipe bomb was detonated in the city's Centennial Olympic Park. More than 100 people were injured with one woman being killed. Not only did Katie and the other *Today* staff in Atlanta have to cover this unexpected and tragic news, but they continued to report on the daily athletic events. As Couric had learned over the decades, in journalism, the unexpected must always be expected.

In the fall of 1996 Katie was busy covering the upcoming presidential elections in which Democratic President Clinton was campaigning against Republican U.S. Senator Bob Dole. Katie attracted a good deal of attention when she posed tough questions to Dole, such as whether his pro-tobacco-industry position had anything to do with their support of his political office seeking. (Her strong, liberal stance against this presidential hopeful was nothing new for Katie, however. Back in 1992 when she interviewed then presidential candidate Ross Perot—running on a third-party ticket—she had so infuriated the mega rich man that he accused her of "trying to prove [her] manhood." Katie, in turn, labeled Perot "the quintessential bully.")

Back at *Today* a major search was in progress to pick a successor to the soon-to-be departing Bryant Gumbel. Having spent nearly six years learning to function as smoothly as possible with the occasionally testy Gumbel, Katie wondered how she would react to, and deal with, her new coanchor.

Suddenly this career concern took a back seat when it was announced that Jeff Zucker, *Today*'s effective chief producer, had been diagnosed with colon cancer. (This disease affects the large intestine. Approximately 138,000 new cases of this form of cancer were being diagnosed each year in the United States and some 55,000 Americans were dying of either colon or rectal cancer.) The news that the 31-year-old Zucker had been stricken deeply affected his network coworkers. It especially hit Katie hard as over the years she had bonded so well with Jeff.

Determined to see her good pal overcome this potentially fatal disease, Katie did what she does best: She researched the facts. She devoted a good deal of her own time investigating the best physicians and latest treatments for this form of cancer that typically struck people over 50. With her newly acquired information, she helped Jeff pick the appropriate specialist. She remained dedicated to Zucker's well being as he underwent cancer surgery and then endured follow-up chemotherapy treatments. Amazingly, within a few months the hard-fighting Zucker returned to his responsibilities at *Today*.

A New TV Partner

As 1996 came to a close, everyone at *Today* prepared for Bryant Gumbel's imminent departure. At one point NBC management suggested that Katie might want to anchor the morning program on her own. She declined that overwhelming responsibility, preferring to share the daily tasks and to have a regular cohost with whom she could interact. Eventually it was decided that Matt Lauer—with his good looks, viewer-friendly and sensitive personality, and solid industry experience—was the right choice for the challenging task. Before Gumbel left in the coming weeks, there was a series of tributes to the departing anchorman, including a special salute on *The Oprah Winfrey Show* in early December 1996. For this episode, Katie, Al Roker (who had replaced Willard Scott as *Today*'s weatherman), and Matt Lauer joined Oprah in an on-air testimonial for the veteran broadcaster.

On January 3, 1997, Gumbel (who was moving over to CBS on a $7 million annual salary), made his final *Today* appearance. Among the emotional on-air farewells from show regulars, Katie read verses she had written about her departing small-screen partner. She finished her cheery but touching poem with "While I've made it clear that you're perfectly sluggable . . . There are times where you are, dare I say it, quite huggable."

If there were any fears at the network or by the public that Katie and Matt would not make a smooth transition, these concerns were soon dispelled. Unlike Bryant Gumbel, Lauer was far more relaxed, easy-going, and amiable on-camera. Avoiding the formal demeanor and look of his predecessor, Matt, a bachelor since his 1988 divorce, seemed content to be a harmonious teammate rather than a leader in on-air partnership with Katie. Hardly had the new cohost begun his chores than Lauer's dad—living in

Florida—told his son he was suffering from a deadly form of lung cancer.

Throughout the next months, until Mr. Lauer passed away, Matt commuted to Florida each weekend to be with his ailing father. How Matt handled this sad personal situation did much to earn him the admiration of *Today* staffers and TV viewers alike. On-camera, Matt did his best to shed his personal problems as he and Katie dealt with serious world issues and lighthearted features.

Katie and Today *cohost Matt Lauer at the 2004 Olympic Games in Athens, Greece* (Getty Images)

Audiences got to see the fun-loving side of Matt in months to come when, on Halloween, he and Al Roker began a tradition of dressing up in costumes to celebrate the holiday. For one year's festivities Roker and Lauer appeared respectively as TV's *Mork and Mindy*; another time they faced the *Today* cameras and the on-street crowd as Puff Daddy and Jennifer Lopez.

Heartache

Ratings continued to mount for the top-rated *Today*. By 1997 more than 10 million people were viewing the daily show around the globe. Meanwhile, Katie's existence continued at a hectic pace, a constant juggling act between work assignments and home life. Increasingly she was receiving recognition for her steady contributions to the well-being of *Today* and for her ongoing accomplishments as a TV journalist. When Valentine's Day arrived in 1997, Procter & Gamble named Couric the winner in a poll for its Scope mouthwash brand, citing Katie as the U.S.'s most kissable famous person.

By now, Jay Monahan had switched into a new career—television. Not only was he a staff legal analyst for the MSNBC cable TV network, but he frequently turned up as a visiting commentator on Geraldo Rivera's nightly TV talk show, *Rivera Live* (CNBC). In both jobs Jay received high marks for his astuteness. No one felt he was merely climbing into the TV arena on the strength of his wife's success within the business.

Jay had been on his new jobs for only a few months when he began experiencing bouts of tiredness and achiness. He attributed these symptoms to the pressures of his new work responsibilities, especially his constant commuting back and forth from New York to Los Angeles to cover the O. J. Simpson civil trial. Then, in April 1997, having postponed seeking medical diagnosis for many weeks because of business demands, Jay finally had a medical exam. He was diagnosed with colon cancer. Unlike Jeff Zucker's colon cancer, which had been detected early on, Jay's condition had already reached an advanced stage.

Katie was staggered by this perilous news. However, she still needed to carry on at work as well as do her best to keep her children calm. She devoted herself to researching the latest treatments and experimental therapies for the disease. On June 6, 1997, Jay underwent surgery followed by a battery of chemotherapy. The medical prognosis was not good, but Jay seemed to respond to the treatments. As soon as possible he insisted upon returning to his own TV chores and to sharing as much time as possible with his wife and youngsters. For Katie, it was an extremely difficult, at times horrible, period. (She said later, "I would wake up every day and say, 'I can't believe Jay got it.'"). She felt relatively helpless as her spouse stubbornly fought against his life-threatening condition.

By the end of 1997, despite every effort made, it was clear that time was running out for Jay. In the new year, a distraught Katie did her best to focus on work, which included interviews with representatives of Monica Lewinsky, a former White House intern alleged to have had an affair with President Clinton. On January 27, 1998, Katie was scheduled to interview first lady Hillary Clinton on *Today*. While Mrs. Clinton planned to talk about child care, a project close to her heart, Katie hoped to broach the delicate subject of the Lewinsky-Clinton scandal.

However, Katie never did this major interview (which was handled by Matt Lauer). On January 24, Jay passed away at New York's Lenox Hill Hospital. He was only 42 years old. On Monday's edition of *Today,* Matt Lauer announced Jay Monahan's death. Many stunned, sympathetic viewers sent messages of sympathy to the grieving Katie. To honor his memory, many individuals made donations to the National Cancer Institute.

A brokenhearted Katie remained away from *Today* as close friends and relatives sought to console her and her two children. To preserve a memory of Jay (especially for their two youngsters), Katie compiled a scrapbook of the many notes she received from those who had known

Jay. These letter-writers, who knew Jay at different points in his relatively short life, shared their joint experiences with Jay with his widow. Katie even received a copy of her husband's college transcripts as well as his college entrance essay. All these became part of her memorial book on Jay.

Picking Up the Pieces

Katie remained away from her TV duties for a month. During this period the show had received thousands of condolence letters and cards for her. On February 24, 1998, the beloved TV figure returned in front of the *Today* cameras. Wearing Jay's wedding ring on a chain around her neck, she addressed the home audience in a dignified manner that was both warm and direct. Her approach was geared to avoid creating the sense that she craved fans' pity. She told viewers, "Words of course, will never describe how devastating this loss has been for me and my daughters . . . and all of Jay's family as well. But the heartfelt and compassionate letters and cards that so many of you have sent to me were enormously comforting, and I'm so grateful."

Matt Lauer, who had endured his own dreadful experience with a close relative suffering from terminal cancer, displayed great compassion when he told Katie with great sincerity and simplicity, "It's great to have you back."

Katie responded by squeezing his hand and thanking him. Then, ever the professional, she proceeded with the day's agenda, which included interviews with U.S. Secretary of State James Baker (in which she discussed strife in Iraq), and a segment where Katie congratulated figure skater Tara Lipinski (who had recently won an Olympic Gold Medal).

Having risen to the occasion on her first day back at work, Katie had to field media efforts to have her address her feelings about Jay's untimely passing. She finally chose to meet with *Newsweek* magazine, telling its reporter, "It's very hard to live out a personal tragedy on national television. . . . Every day my heart was breaking." She went on to explain that her pain and grief were very private matters that could not be shared with the public. It was only many weeks after losing her husband that she could bring herself to talk about her pain in a public forum. While accepting an award that June from Avon Women of Enterprise, she said to the audience gathered in New York City: "How do you go on when fate delivers such a crushing blow that it causes permanent damage to your heart?" She continued her compelling speech with, "People ask how and why do you go on and do what you have to do. I do it because I have two girls who are depending on me to show them what you have to do when life throws you a major curve ball."

Later, for the October 1998 issue of *Good Housekeeping* magazine, Katie told writer Joanna Powell that in the aftershock of Jay's death, "I went through a period when I was just impossible to deal with. Because I was just so, so upset and angry and furious with the world." She acknowledged that in this crisis time she had turned to her parents: "Talk about unconditional love they've always been there for me." On another occasion, for the April 2000 issue of *McCall's*, Katie said that throughout the whole recovery process she always kept her children's welfare in mind. "I let them know that their mommy was still here, still able to take care of things. That is really my greatest accomplishment. . . ."

Being a constructive doer by nature, Katie wanted Jay's passing to bring about positive changes for others who might possibly find themselves in his medical situation. Having amassed (with the help of *Today* staffers) a tremendous amount of research on the subject of colon cancer, she prepared a weeklong series on the subject, which was aired on *Today* that September. Portions of the coverage were reused on other NBC/MSNBC news programs.

Next, Katie joined with Lilly Tartikoff (whose TV/film executive husband Brandon had died of cancer in 1997) to form the National Colorectal Cancer Research Alliance (NCCRA), part of the Entertainment Industry Foundation.

Because of the passionate efforts of the co-founders and their many supporters, over subsequent years the NCCRA raised many millions of dollars to fund additional research into colon and rectal cancer—its diagnosis, treatment, and potential cure. For Katie this activity became a mainstay of her life as she worked tirelessly advocating colon cancer education. She especially wanted to alert the public at large of the need for periodic examinations to detect the possible start of the disease so that it could be prevented from spreading to a fatal level. In this period Katie also founded the Jay Monahan Center for Gastrointestinal Health in New York.

Being in Demand

Slowly recovering from her husband's death, Katie realized that, as a single parent, she now was fully responsible for her family's welfare. She sold the Virginia farm that she and Jay had so cherished, knowing that now she would be largely based in Manhattan. On the other hand she kept the house that she and her husband had purchased in upstate New York. This retreat afforded all the benefits of being in the countryside without being too isolated from neighbors.

Taking another positive step, she purchased a spacious and sunny apartment in New York City. Always thrifty but wanting the new home to be especially warm and comfortable for the girls and to provide a relaxed environment for herself, she redecorated the new home with a bright and cheerful décor. In the dining room she placed the life-sized mannequin of a nineteenth-century soldier that Monahan had purchased only weeks before his death. (This decorating touch made Katie and the children feel as if Jay was there watching over them.)

With her newly refurbished residence complete, Katie proudly showed friends and the media through the apartment. In guiding one such interviewer through her new residence, Katie looked around at the well-furnished rooms and observed, "I feel like I've grown up. This is a grown-up apartment."

7

A MIGHTY MEDIA FORCE

In the spring of 1998, while Katie Couric was still adjusting to the loss of her husband and regaining her momentum at *Today*, her NBC employers were concerned that she might leave *Today* when her contract expired in the coming months. Thus they entered into high-level negotiations with Katie's representatives to keep her at the network for the next several years.

According to entertainment industry trade publications in June 1998, NBC first offered to raise Katie's salary to about $4 million a year. (At the time, ABC's Peter Jennings, Ted Koppel, and Diane Sawyer, CBS's Dan Rather, and NBC's Tom Brokaw were each earning about $7 million yearly; ABC's Barbara Walters was drawing a $10 million annual income.) It was rumored that Couric was unhappy with NBC's offer and was threatening to leave *Today*. By late June, the network bid had risen to a $7 million annual package for the star newscaster/interviewer.

While Katie refused to confirm the exact amount of her new NBC deal, she told *Newsweek* magazine, "You want me to justify my salary? I thought you might ask me about that. Because I'm one of those people who wonders about the distortion in salaries in this country—why pro-basketball players make this outrageous sum of money and teachers don't make much at all. But having said that . . . my personality plays a role in the show's success, not that it would collapse if I left. But people have this strong connection to you and form these bonds with you that are almost familial. It takes a long time to win the audience's trust and affection. Maintaining that continuity I think accounts for the way I'm compensated."

Even with her enormous income, Katie remained her prudent self. She explained, "My parents are children of the Depression. . . . It rubbed off. I think I'm very generous with my friends. But I worry about spending money. . . . I am frugal. But without getting too psychobabbly, it's my way of maintaining a sense that I'm just like everyone else. [*Today*'s executive producer] Jeff Zucker said that with my new contract I could probably fly first class. I said, 'Even for personal trips?'"

The Award Winner

Having won recognition of her worth from her network bosses, Katie also received several new awards for her professional abilities and the regard in which the public held her. In its "Most Admired Women Poll" *Good Housekeeping* cited Katie as the top journalist. *Life* magazine selected Katie to be among its "Heroes of the Year," citing the dignity that she displayed while dealing with her husband's death. Later she received the "All American Hero" Award from the Fresh Air Fund.

On April 22, 1999, Katie was on hand in Littleton, Colorado to interview distraught family members of some of the 13 people who had died in a shooting at Columbine High School. Following the difficult interview, Matt Lauer commented from the *Today* studio, "Katie, I don't think I've ever seen a more compelling and emotional interview than the one you just conducted. . . . "

In March 2000 Katie, the anti-colon cancer crusader, went to Washington, D.C., to appear before the U.S. Senate Select Committee on Aging. There she publicized the "need for greater awareness and more widespread screening" regarding colon and rectal cancer. She also placed on the record a progress report of the work being accomplished by the National Colorectal Cancer Research Alliance, for which she had been a cofounder.

Katie testified before the Senate Special Committee on Aging in 2000 to discuss the importance of colorectal cancer screening tests. The disease claimed the life of her husband, Jay, in 1998. (Associated Press)

Also in March 2000, Katie, who was featured on the cover of *Time* magazine (March 13, 2000), took a very bold step in her ongoing campaign to educate the public about colon cancer. On the *Today* show Katie underwent an actual colonoscopy, an invasive test used to examine the colon for polyps or other possible signs of cancer.

This graphic, informative TV presentation had a tremendous positive impact on many millions of home viewers. In the coming months the medical profession recorded a nationwide jump of 20 percent in the number of Americans who underwent a colonoscopy exam. Soon doctors—and the media—were referring to this boost in testing as the "Couric Effect." For her highly regarded colon-test series, Katie later won not only an Emmy Award but also a prestigious Peabody Award. However, the greatest reward for her extensive labors on behalf of colon cancer education is the fact that her efforts have helped so many individuals. Katie says, "Almost every day, I get a letter from someone who says, 'I got screened for colon cancer because of you. You saved my life.' It doesn't get any better than that."

Coming Alive Again

Two years after Jay Monahan's death, Katie felt emotionally ready to date again. Hesitant about upsetting her young children, Katie kept such activity low-key. One of her frequent escorts soon became Tom Werner, the extremely wealthy coproducer of several successful TV sitcoms such as *The Cosby Show, Roseanne,* and *3rd Rock From the Sun,* as well as a co-owner of the baseball team the Boston Red Sox. Seven years older than Katie, Tom was also the father of three children and was then in the midst of a divorce. Because Werner was based on the West Coast and Katie in New York City and each had demanding work schedules, it was often difficult for the couple to spend sufficient time together. This was a key factor in their seesawing relationship over the coming years.

While Katie was attempting to get her life back in balance in these years, she faced another personal tragedy. In July 2000 her elder sister Emily was diagnosed with pancreatic cancer. At the time, Emily was a state senator in Virginia. She was a rising personality within the Democratic Party and was projected to run for lieutenant governor of the state. After discovering her ailment, Emily dropped out of the race. While continuing in the Senate, she assumed the role of co-chair of the state party. In October 2001, Emily died at the age of 54, leaving family and friends grief-stricken.

Becoming an Author

With Katie's many talents and driving energy it was not too surprising when it was announced that she was turning to fiction writing of children's books. (Katie had already provided introductions and commentary on several adult books dealing with such topics as health and childrearing.) According to Katie, "I started to write this book in my spare time. I would write bits and pieces on Saturday mornings before my children were awake, because my body clock is such that I get up early." On another occasion, she explained to *Parenting* magazine, "I have this terrible need to always be doing something. . . . So I just got started and then there was no turning back." She also mentioned, "I like writing little ditties, and I have some things I want to say about helping kids, so I thought that it would be fun to translate those into a book."

In this tale for youngsters (illustrated by Marjorie Priceman), the two lead characters—Ellie McSnelly and Carrie O'Toole (named after Katie's daughters)—are second-graders who befriend a new classmate, a recent arrival from Hungary. Although the other schoolmates make fun of this foreigner, Ellie and Carrie show compassion for the boy. Katie explained of her book's theme: "I'm hoping that kids will become more aware and that they may reach out to those who are different from them."

Titled *The Brand New Kid,* Katie's book was published by Doubleday in October 2000 and also appeared in a Spanish-language edition (*El Niño Nuevo*). The well-received book led Katie to write other books, including

Katie holds a copy of the first children's book she wrote, The Brand New Kid. *(WireImage)*

The Blue Ribbon Day (2004). This new publication again featured Ellie and Carrie who, this time, are trying out for the school's soccer team. When only one of them is chosen for the squad it causes temporary difficulties in their friendship. The inspiring story was geared to provide young readers with a lesson in building self-confidence.

On a more serious note, Katie would also provide an introduction for such other books as *What Your Doctor May Not Tell You About Colorectal Cancer: New Tests, New Treatments, New Hope* (2004) and *Tales from the Bed: On Living, Dying and Having It All* (2004). The latter entry concerned Couric's friend, New York stage producer Jenifer Estess who, at age 40, died following a valiant six-year struggle with ALS (Lou Gehrig's disease).

A New Katie

As Katie emerged from her mourning for Jay, she decided she could use a fresh look to welcome the new millennium. She worked with a personal trainer, revamped her wardrobe (getting away from suits), and altered her hairstyle and color. The superstar TV news figure joked about her revitalized, sophisticated appearance by saying, "I think the statute of limitations on perky ran out three years ago."

Katie's participation on *Today* proceeded at the same high pace, but now included helping the expanded daily show (now three hours) to fill its air time with additional material. She continued to conduct controversial interviews, such as her August 2001 talk with the mother and brother of confessed child murderer Andrea Yates. With such topical, often thought-provoking pieces, she kept herself—and *Today*—high in viewers' popularity. When the nation and the world was thunderstruck by the terrorist attacks on the World Trade Center and Pentagon on September 11, 2001, Katie was one of the many media journalists who remained on the air all day helping TV viewers to process the astounding news and its tragic aftermath.

Katie's continued appeal to TV watchers was a constant source of interest to rival networks and producers. In the last months of 2001, many of *Today*'s competitors began seriously courting Katie, whom *TV Guide* had named Best News Person of the Year. Katie's corporate suitors hoped that when her NBC News contract expired the following May, she might switch over to their shows. Top companies angled to make Katie—then listed by *Entertainment Weekly*'s annual survey as number 11 of the industry's "100 Most Powerful People"—part of their team.

Jeffrey Katzenberg and Steven Spielberg at the film studio DreamWorks were pursuing Katie to host a syndicated TV talk show for their film studio. They spent over $100,000 on an elaborate video production that included having a large group of extras waving signs that read "We Love You Katie." Katzenberg was so excited by the potential of Couric coming aboard that he wrote out a multi-million dollar check, which he handed to the star's representatives. They were told that this was a bonus if Katie signed with DreamWorks. AOL-Time Warner was another important contender. That media giant wanted Katie for a nationwide talk show, a website, and a *Time* magazine column. Yet another major company that courted Couric was CBS News, which offered her a slot on *60 Minutes* or another of the network's successful news magazine programs.

Everyone wondered what Katie would do next professionally. However, by late December 2001 Katie had signed a five-year extension with *Today* at a $65 million fee. Now earning $13 million per year, Katie was receiving, according to the *Washington Post*, a salary 30 percent higher than Tom Brokaw and $1 million more annually than Barbara Walters. Katie's cohost Matt Lauer was then earning a reported $4 million annually.

When asked what had prompted her to participate in this "battle for Katie Couric," the TV personality said, "Some of the offers did intrigue me. I felt I owed it to myself to see what else was out there, and there were some exciting-sounding things." In the long run, however, she determined that many of the suggested opportunities

Harry Potter *author, J.K. Rowling, with Katie* (Photofest)

would have meant relocating to California and/or required too much traveling. She decided such options would be unfair to her two girls. Besides, having spent so many years with *Today*, she felt "The prospect of leaving NBC made me a little sick to my stomach." She added, "I learned that I do love my job as much as I thought. That was very comforting."

Facing *Today*'s Tomorrows

While Katie was bargaining with NBC about remaining with *Today*, the show itself was undergoing changes. Long-time (executive) producer Jeff Zucker had already moved on to become President of NBC Entertainment. Thereafter, Jonathan Wald became executive producer of NBC's popular morning show. However, in November 2002 Wald was replaced by Tom Touchet because, according to *Mediaweek*, there had been disagreements between Wald and *Today*'s coanchors. With all these management changes and the aggressiveness of its early morning TV competition, *Today* was losing some of its ratings edge to *Good Morning America* and *CBS Morning News*.

In November 2002 Katie encountered disappointing ratings when she hosted *Katie at Night*, a prime-time celebrity profile show. Katie did much better with her hard-news stories, such as her Emmy Award–nominated evening special in April 2003, in which she interviewed the victim in Manhattan's notorious Central Park jogger rape case. The next month, she and late-night talk host Jay Leno switched jobs for one day. This network-stage gimmick boosted the ratings of their adopted shows. (Katie proved especially adept in handling Leno's entertainment format.) As one of the hosts for NBC's coverage of the Macy's Thanksgiving Day Parade in November 2003, Katie later shared a Daytime Emmy win.

In October 2003, Katie hosted a nighttime special devoted to a talk with Utah teenager Elizabeth Smart (who had been freed after being held hostage by kidnappers for nine months) and her family. Later that same month, Katie, along with game show host Bob Barker, actor/comedian Art Carney, TV news journalist Dan Rather, and the late industry executive Brandon Tartikoff were selected as the latest inductees into the Academy of Television Arts & Sciences' Hall of Fame. In announcing the selections, Dick Askin, chairman of the organization stated, "Certainly, the extraordinary bodies of work [of these individuals] have each helped shape our industry and serve as benchmarks for excellence for all people involved in our craft."

As Katie moved into 2004, her thirteenth year with *Today*, she was in top form as she interviewed a variety of political and entertainment figures. The veteran talent admitted publicly that there were some work-related activities she had done when she was younger (e.g., going to the trouble zone twice during the 1991 Persian Gulf War) that she would not do these days (e.g., visiting war-torn Iraq, although she did visit troops in nearby Saudi Arabia). She explained, "Now I just wouldn't risk it. It's too dangerous. I'm a single parent. There are things I will not do for my job, and one of them is risk my life."

To provide more airtime and prestige for some of her key new interviews, Katie conducted these Q&A sessions

Katie's career has taken her on assignments all over the world. Here she interviews a member of the U.S. Navy in Saudi Arabia during the Iraq War. (Getty Images)

on NBC's *Dateline*. This included Katie's June 2004 sit down with O. J. Simpson, on the tenth anniversary of his double-murder case. However, the light side of Katie Couric was never out of viewer sight for too long, as when, in July 2004, she was shown on *Today* engaging in a game of badminton. Meanwhile, just as she had made a cameo appearance as a prison guard in the comedic theatrical release *Austin Powers: Goldmember* (2002), she also provided the voice of the character Katie Current for the 2004 animated film *Shark Tale.*

Looking Back and Ahead

When Katie was queried if she will continue to remain at her high-paying *Today* job after her 2006 contract expiration, she says, "At some point, I'm going to want a new challenge. But it's hard, when you love your job so much, to think about a) giving it up and b) what's next. I do want to make sure that I'm out there doing some good in the world."

Not long ago Katie Couric was asked for a *Reader's Digest* profile whether her great professional success surprised her. She responded, "I feel like I've accomplished a lot, but this is not the stuff that makes you happy ultimately. It's your relationships, your children, giving back, and all those things that sound so corny. I love having an exciting professional life. And it has well exceeded my wildest expectations. I still think it's hilarious. Sometimes I'll talk to people I knew early on in my career, and we'll say, 'Can you believe this happened?'"

TIME LINE

1957 Born in Arlington, Virginia, on January 7, the last of four children

1975 Graduates from Yorktown High School in Arlington; begins studies at University of Virginia in Charlottesville; interns at local radio stations during summers

1979 Earns a B.A. degree with honors from the University of Virginia; starts career in broadcast journalism as desk assistant at ABC-TV's News bureau in Washington, D.C.

1980 Hired as assignment editor by CNN at its Washington office

1982 Relocates to Atlanta, Georgia to be producer (and, unofficially, occasional on-air reporter) on the CNN daily program, *Take Two*

1984 Temporary political correspondent for CNN's coverage of the presidential campaign; joins station WTVJ in Miami as a general assignment reporter; multi-part feature on child pornography wins local industry award

1986 Back again in Washington, D.C., working for station WRC-TV, a NBC network affiliate, as a general assignment reporter

1989 Feature piece on dating service for the handicapped earns regional Emmy trophy and Associated Press Award; joins NBC News as deputy Pentagon reporter; weds attorney Jay Monahan

1990 Takes on post of national correspondent for NBC-TV's *Today* program based in Washington, D.C.

1991 Joins *Today* in New York City as Bryant Gumbel's new coanchor; gives birth to first child, Elinor Tully Monahan

1992 As part of *Today* assignments reports on Summer Olympics in Barcelona, Spain and on U.S. presidential race; White House tour with First Lady Barbara Bush leads to spontaneous interview with President George Bush; negotiates new *Today* pact worth over $1 million annually

1993 Adds to broadcast chores by becoming coanchor of NBC's evening magazine format show, *Now with Tom Brokaw and Katie Couric*

1994 When *Now* is folded into NBC's *Dateline* primetime series, becomes contributing anchor while continuing at *Today*; Jay Monahan relocates full time to Manhattan, working at a New York law firm

1996 Reports on Summer Olympics in Atlanta, Georgia and November presidential race; *Today* producer/close friend Jeff Zucker undergoes treatment for colon cancer prompting Katie's initial research on the disease; gives birth to second child, Caroline Couric Monahan

1997 Cohost Bryant Gumbel departs *Today* and is replaced by Matt Lauer; Jay Monahan is diagnosed with advanced colon cancer

1998 Jay Monahan dies of colon cancer; Katie creates highly-regarded colon cancer education series for *Today*; cofounds the National Colorectal Cancer Research Alliance (NCCRA) and starts Jay Monahan Center for Gastrointestinal Health; signs new *Today* contract for $7 million yearly; purchases a Manhattan apartment

1999 Reports from Littleton, Colorado on shootings at Columbine High School; receives several awards, including *Good Housekeeping* magazine's "Most Admired Women" and *Life*'s "Hero of the Year"

2000 *Today*, now in 48th year, expands to three-hour format; elder sister Emily, a Virginia state senator, is diagnosed with pancreatic cancer; has on-air colonoscopy exam as part of award-winning series on colon cancer; dates veteran TV producer Tom Werner. Book: *The Brand New Kid*.

2001 Reports on terrorists' attack on World Trade Center; signs new five-year *Today* agreement, valued at over $13 million yearly; named "Best News Person of the Year" by *TV Guide*; sister Emily dies

2002 Hosts *Katie at Night*, a celebrity interview TV special. Film: *Austin Powers: Goldmember* (New Line)

2003 Interview with Central Park Jogger earns Couric a Primetime Emmy Award nomination; she and late-night TV talk show host Jay Leno switch jobs for one day

2004 Primetime interview with O. J. Simpson; reports on presidential race; shares Daytime Emmy win for NBC's coverage of Macy's Thanksgiving Day Parade.

Books: *The Blue Ribbon Day*; introduction for *Tales from the Bed: On Living, Dying, and Having It All* and foreword for *What Your Doctor May Not Tell You About Colorectal Cancer: New Tests, New Treatments, New Hope*. Film: *Shark Tale* (DreamWorks)

2005 Hosts prime-time NCB-TV special *The 411: Teens and Sex*

HOW TO BECOME A NEWS BROADCASTER

THE JOB

News broadcasters, also called news anchors, specialize in presenting the news to the listening or viewing public. They report the facts and may sometimes be asked to provide editorial commentary. They may write their own scripts or rely on the station's writing team to write the script that they then read over the TelePrompTer. Research is important to each news story and the news broadcasters should be well informed about each story they cover as well as those they simply introduce. News broadcasters may also report the news, produce special segments, and conduct on-the-air interviews and panel discussions. At small stations, they may even keep the program log, run the transmitter, and cue the changeover to network broadcasting.

News broadcasters are faced with constant deadlines, not only for each newscast to begin, but also for each one to end. Each segment must be viewed and each script must be read at the precise time and for a specified duration during the newscast. While they must appear calm, professional, and confident, there is often much stress and tension behind the scenes.

Although they perform similar jobs, radio and television news broadcasters work in very different atmospheres. On radio, the main announcers or anchor people are also the *disc jockeys.* They play recorded music, announce the news, provide informal commentary, and serve as a bridge between the music and the listener. They announce the time, weather, news, and traffic reports while maintaining a cheerful and relaxed attitude. At most stations, the radio announcers also read advertising information or provide the voices for the advertising spots.

For *television news anchors,* research, writing, and presenting the news is only part of the job. The TV news anchor's wardrobe, makeup, and overall look are vital in conveying the correct tone for the broadcast; getting physically ready for the day is an important part of an anchor's job. Many details such as which hairstyles and which outfits to wear are important to create an effective look for the news.

Some radio or television news broadcasters specialize in certain aspects of the news such as health, economics, politics, or community affairs. Other broadcasters specialize in sports. These people cover sports events and must be highly knowledgeable about the sports they are covering as well as having an ability to describe events quickly and accurately as they unfold. *Sports anchors* generally travel to the events they cover and spend time watching the teams or individuals practice and participate. They research background information, statistics, ratings, and personal interest information to provide the audience with the most thorough and interesting coverage of each sports event.

The Internet and the World Wide Web are changing the job of news broadcasters in radio and television. Many radio and television stations have their own websites where listeners and viewers can keep updated on current stories, email their comments and suggestions, and even interact with the anchors and reporters. Also, the World Wide Web has become another resource for broadcasters as they research their stories.

Because their voices and faces are heard and seen by the public on a daily basis, many radio and television news broadcasters become well-known public personalities. This means that they are often asked to participate in community activities and other public events.

REQUIREMENTS

High School

In high school, you should focus on a college preparatory curriculum that will teach you how to write and speak and use the English language in literature and communication classes. Subjects such as history, government, economics, and a foreign language are also important. Participation in journalism clubs and on your school newspaper will also help you prepare for this career.

Postsecondary Training

Today, most news broadcasters have earned at least a bachelor's degree in journalism, English, political science, economics, telecommunications, or communications. Visit the website (http://www.ku.edu/~acejmc/STUDENT/PROGLIST.SHTML) of the Accrediting Council on Education in Journalism and Mass Communications for a list of accredited postsecondary training programs in journalism and mass communications.

Other Requirements

Aspiring radio and television news broadcasters must have a mastery of the English language—both written and spoken. Their diction, including correct grammar usage, pronunciation, and lack of regional dialect, is extremely important. News broadcasters need to have a pleasing personality and voice, and, in the case of television anchor people, they must also have a pleasing appearance.

News broadcasters need to be creative, inquisitive, aggressive, and should know how to meet and interact with people—including coworkers and people whom they interview to help gather the news.

EXPLORING

If you are interested in a career as a news anchor, try to get a summer job at a radio or television station. Although you will probably not have the opportunity to broadcast, you may be able to judge whether or not the type of work appeals to you as a career.

Any chance to speak or perform before an audience should be welcomed. Join the speech or debate team to build strong speaking skills. Appearing as a speaker or performer can show whether or not you have the stage presence necessary for a career in front of a microphone or camera.

Many colleges and universities have their own radio and television stations and offer courses in radio and television. You can gain valuable experience working at college-owned stations. Some radio stations, cable systems, and TV stations offer financial assistance, internships, and co-op work programs, as well as scholarships and fellowships.

EMPLOYERS

Of the roughly 76,000 announcers (including news broadcasters) working in the United States, almost all are on staff at one of the 13,563 radio stations or 1,733 television stations around the country. Some, however, work on a freelance basis on individual assignments for networks, stations, advertising agencies, and other producers of commercials.

Some companies own several television or radio stations; some stations belong to networks such as ABC, CBS, NBC, or FOX, while others are independent. While radio and television stations are located throughout the United States, major markets where better-paying jobs are found are generally near large metropolitan areas.

STARTING OUT

Most news broadcasters start in jobs such as production assistant, researcher, or reporter in small stations. As opportunities arise, it is common for broadcasters to move from one job to another. Network jobs are few, and the competition for them is great. You must have several years of experience as well as a college education to be considered for these positions.

You must audition before you will be employed as a news anchor. You should carefully select audition material to show a prospective employer the full range of your abilities. In addition to presenting prepared materials, you may be asked to read material that you have not seen previously, such as a commercial, news release, dramatic selection, or poem.

ADVANCEMENT

Radio and television news broadcasters move up by moving on. In other words, one of the main ways to advance within the industry is to move to a larger market or larger station. The ultimate goal of many news broadcasters is to advance to the network level. Others advance by becoming news directors, station managers, or producers.

EARNINGS

According to the *2002 Radio and Television Salary Survey* by the Radio-Television News Directors Association, there is a wide range of salaries for news broadcasters. For radio news broadcasters, the median salary was $27,500 with a low of $10,000 and a high of $150,000. For television news broadcasters, the median salary was $50,000 with a low of $17,000 and a high of $1 million. The highest profile news broadcasters command multimillion-dollar salaries, but they are the exception.

Median annual earnings of all announcers (including news broadcasters) were $20,940 in 2003, according to the U.S. Department of Labor. Salaries ranged from less than $12,750 to $52,560 or more.

For both radio and television, salaries are higher in the larger markets. Salaries are also generally higher in commercial than in public broadcasting. Nationally known news broadcasters who appear regularly on network television programs receive salaries that may be quite impressive. For those who become top television personalities in large metropolitan areas, salaries also are quite high.

WORK ENVIRONMENT

Work in radio and television stations is usually very pleasant. Almost all stations are housed in modern facilities. The maintenance of technical electronic equipment requires temperature and dust control, and people who work around such equipment benefit from the precautions taken to preserve it.

News broadcasters' jobs may provide opportunities to meet well-known people or celebrities. Being at the center of an important communications medium can make the broadcaster more keenly aware of current issues and divergent points of view than the average person.

News broadcasters may report for work at a very early hour in the morning or work late into the night. Some radio stations operate on a 24-hour basis. All-night news broadcasters may be alone in the station during their working hours.

OUTLOOK

Competition for entry-level employment in announcing during the coming years is expected to be keen, as the broadcasting industry always attracts more applicants than are needed to fill available openings. There is a better chance of working in radio than in television because there are more radio stations. Local television stations usually carry a high percentage of network programs and need only a very small staff to carry out local operations.

The U.S. Department of Labor predicts that opportunities for announcers (including news broadcasters) will decline through 2012 due to the slowing growth of new radio and television stations. Openings will result mainly from those who leave the industry or the labor force. The trend among major networks, and to some extent among many smaller radio and TV stations, is toward specialization. News broadcasters who specialize in such areas as business, sports, weather, consumer, and health news should have an advantage over other job applicants.

TO LEARN MORE ABOUT NEWS BROADCASTERS

BOOKS

Freedman, Wayne. *It Takes More Than Good Looks to Succeed at TV News Reporting.* Chicago: Bonus Books, 2003.

Kalbfeld, Brad. *The Associated Press Broadcast News Handbook.* New York: McGraw-Hill, 2001.

Keller, Teresa, and Stephen A. Hawkins. *Television News: A Handbook for Writing, Reporting, Shooting, and Editing.* Scottsdale, Ariz.: Holcomb Hathaway, 2001.

McCoy, Michelle, and Ann S. Utterback. *Sound and Look Professional on Television and the Internet: How to Improve Your On-Camera Presence.* Chicago: Bonus Books, 2000

FOR MORE INFORMATION

For a list of accredited programs in journalism and mass communications, visit the ACEJMC website.

Accrediting Council on Education in Journalism and Mass Communications (ACEJMC)
University of Kansas School of Journalism and Mass Communications,
Stauffer-Flint Hall, 1435 Jayhawk Boulevard
Lawrence, KS 66045
http://www.ku.edu/~acejmc/STUDENT/PROGLIST.SHTML

For a list of schools offering degrees in broadcasting as well as scholarship information, contact
Broadcast Education Association
1771 N Street, NW
Washington, DC 20036
Tel: 888-380-7222
Email: beainfo@beaweb.org
http://www.beaweb.org

To Learn More about News Broadcasters • 111

For college programs and union information, contact
National Association of Broadcast Employees and Technicians
501 Third Street, NW, 8th Floor
Washington, DC 20001
Tel: 202-434-1254
Email: nabet@nabetcwa.org
http://nabetcwa.org

For broadcast education and scholarship information, contact
National Association of Broadcasters
1771 N Street, NW
Washington, DC 20036
Tel: 202-429-5300
Email: nab@nab.org
http://www.nab.org

For information on farm broadcasting, contact
National Association of Farm Broadcasters
PO Box 500
Platte City, MO 64079
Tel: 816-431-4032
http://www.nafb.com

For scholarship and internship information, contact
Radio-Television News Directors Association
Radio-Television News Directors Foundation
1600 K Street, NW, Suite 700
Washington, DC 20006
Tel: 202-659-6510
Email: rtnda@rtnda.org
http://www.rtnda.org

For comprehensive information for citizens, students, and news people about the field of journalism, visit
Project for Excellence in Journalism and the Committee of Concerned Journalists
http://www.journalism.org

TO LEARN MORE ABOUT KATIE COURIC

BOOKS

Couric, Katherine. *The Blue Ribbon Day*. New York: Doubleday, 2004.*

_____. *The Brand New Kid*. New York: Doubleday, 2000.*

Estess, Jennifer, as told to Valerie Estess, introduction by Katie Couric. *Tales from the Bed: On Living, Dying, and Having It All*. New York: Atria, 2004.

Hack, Richard. *Madness in the Morning: Life and Death in TV's Early Morning Ratings War*. Los Angeles: New Millennium, 1999.

Kessler, Judy. *Inside Today: The Battle for the Morning*. New York: Random House, 1992.

Mink, Eric. *This Is Today: A Window on Our Times.* Kansas City, Mo.: Andrews McMeel, 2003.

Paprocki, Sherry Beck. *Katie Couric*. Philadelphia: Chelsea House, 1991.**

Pochapin, Mark, with foreword by Katie Couric. *What Your Doctor May Not Tell You About Colorectal Cancer: New Tests, New Treatments, New Hope.* New York: Warner, 2004.

* Children's Book
** Young Adult Book

WEBSITES

About Talk Shows
http://talkshows.about.com/od/katiecouric

E! Online
http://www.eonline.com

Internet Movie Database
http://www.imdb.com

The Jay Monahan Center for Gastrointestinal Health
http://www.monahancenter.org/

The Katie Couric Connection
http://www.anemali.net/katie/connection.html

***Larry King Live* Transcripts**
http://www.cnn.com/TRANSCRIPTS/lkl.html

MSNBC Network
http://www.msnbc.com

National Colorectal Cancer Research Alliance
http://www.eifoundation.org/national/nccra/splash

NBC Network
http://www.nbc.com

INDEX

Page numbers in *italics* indicate illustrations.

A

ABC 35, 104
    Couric at 14–16, 93
ABC Evening News (TV program) 14–16
Academy of Television Arts & Sciences' Hall of Fame 88
Accrediting Council on Education in Journalism and Mass Communications (ACEJMC) 102, 110
AOL-Time Warner 85
Askin, Dick 88
Austin Powers: Goldmember (film) 90, 96
Avon Women of Enterprise 71

B

Baker, James 71
Barker, Bob 88
Blue Ribbon Day, The (Couric) 83, 97
Boston Red Sox 80
Brand New Kid, The (Couric) 81, *82,* 96
Broadcast Education Association 110
Brokaw, Tom 1, 35, 39, 52, 58, 75, 85
Brown, Nicole 59
Bush, Barbara 48–49, 94
Bush, George H. W. 49–50, 54–55, 94

C

cancer, colon and rectal 63–64, 68–69, 72–73, 95, 96
Carney, Art 88
Castro, Fidel 20
Cavalier Daily 12
CBS 104
    headquartered in New York 14
    Rather at 1, 75

CBS Morning News (TV program) 47, 87
CBS News 85
Chancellor, John 34
Cheers (TV program) 51
Chung, Connie 5, 54
Clinton, Bill 56, 63, 69
Clinton, Hillary Rodham 51, 69
CNBC 67
CNN
   Couric at 16–21, 93–94
Columbia Lighthouse for the Blind 10, 11
Columbine High School shooting 77, 96
Cosby Show, The (TV program) 80
Couric, Clara "Kiki" (sister) 7, 13, 15
Couric, Elinor (mother) 7, 8, 9
Couric, Emily (sister) 7, 8, 12–13, 80, 96
Couric, John (brother) 7, 13
Couric, John (father) 7, 8, 12, 28
Couric, Katherine Anne "Katie" *3, 56, 86, 89*
   at ABC 14–16, 93
   as author 80–83, *82*
   awards won by 22, 23, 67, 71, 77, 79, 84, 88, 94, 96
   birth 7, 93
   books about 113–114
   childhood 8–9
   children 44, *45,* 56–57, 59, 68, 69–70, 71, 72, 73–74, 79, 81, 87, 89, 90, 94, 95
   at CNN 16–21, 93–94
   at college 11–12, 14, *15,* 93
   on colon and rectal cancer research 72–73, 77–79, *78*
   courtship and marriage 27–30, *29,* 52–53, 94
   husband's illness and death 68–74, 95
   industry record set by 1–4
   journalistic concerns of 4
   at NBC 1–4, 21–26, 30–31, 36–44, *37,* 46–52, 53–54, 55–56, 57–59, 61–64, 65, 66, *66,* 67, 69, 70–71, 72, 75–77, 79, 83–91, *89,* 94–97
   salary 1–2, 43, 47, 75–76, 85, 94, 95, 96
   teenage years 10–11, 93
   time line 93–97
   on Walters *13,* 13–14
   wardrobe of 40, 61–62, 83
   on websites 114–115
   at WRC 22–24, 26, 94
   at WTVJ 21–22, 94
Curle, Chris 17, 18, 19, 21, 54

D

Dateline (TV program) 52, 54, 89–90, 95
disc jockeys 100
Doctor, Dianne 4–5
Dole, Bob 63
Donaldson Sam 15–16
Downs, Hugh 34, 35
DreamWorks 84, 85

E

Ebersol, Dick 36

Entertainment Industry Foundation 72
Entertainment Weekly 50–51, 84
E! Online 114
Estess, Jenifer 83
Eye to Eye (TV program) 54

F

Farmer, Don 18, 19, 21
411, The: Teens and Sex (TV special) 97
FOX 104
Francis, Fred 24–25, 26
Fresh Air Fund 77

G

Garroway, Dave 34
Gartner, Michael 2–4
George 55
Georgetown Law Journal 27
Georgetown University Law School 27
Goldman, Ronald 57, 59
Good Housekeeping 15, 72, 77, 96
Goodman, Walter 37–38
Good Morning America (TV program) 35, 41, 47, 87
Gumbel, Bryant 35–36, 37, 38, *39*, 40, 41, 48, 51, 55, 57, 58, 59, 63, 64, 65, 94, 95

H

Harding, Tonya 57
Home (TV program) 33
Hunton and Williams 52
Hussein, king of Jordan 41

I

Internet 101
Internet Movie Database 114
Iowa, USS (ship) 25
Iran Contra Affair 49

J

Jay Monahan Center for Gastrointestinal Health, The 73, 95, 114
Jefferson, Thomas 12
Jennings, Peter 1, 75

K

Katie at Night (TV program) 87, 96
Katie Couric Connection, The 115
Katzenberg, Jeffrey 84–85
Kerrigan, Nancy 57
Kitman, Marvin 38
Koppel, Ted 1, 75

L

Larry King Live transcripts 115
Lauer, Matt 1, 58, 59, 64–67, *66*, 69, 70–71, 77, 85, 95
Leader, Tammi 21
Legend to Legend Night: A Celebrity Cavalcade (TV special) 52
Leno, Jay 88, 96
Lewinsky, Monica 69
Life 77, 96
Lipinski, Tara 71
Lunden, Joan 5

M

Macy's Thanksgiving Day Parade 88, 96
Marcus, Bret 24
McCall's 72
Mediaweek 87
Monahan, Caroline Couric "Carrie" (daughter) 59, 62, 95
Monahan, Elinor Tully "Ellie" (daughter) 44, *45,* 56–57, 94
Monahan, John Paul III "Jay" (husband)
    children 44, 59
    courtship and marriage 27–30, *29,* 43, 52–53, 55, 94
    illness and death 68–74, 95
    legal work 27–28, 44, 52–53, 67–68
Mondale, Walter 20
Mork and Mindy (TV program) 67
MSNBC 67, 72, 115
Muggs, J. Fred 34
Murphy, Mary 47
Murphy Brown (TV program) 51

N

National Association of Broadcast Employees and Technicians 111
National Association of Broadcasters 111
National Association of Farm Broadcasters 111
National Cancer Institute 69
National Colorectal Cancer Research Alliance (NCCRA) 72–73, 77, 95, 115
NBC 104
    Couric at 1–4, 21–26, 30–31, 36–44, *37,* 46–52, 53–54, 55–56, 57–59, 61–64, 65, 66, *66,* 67, 69, 70–71, 72, 75–77, 79, 83–91, *89,* 94–97
    website of 115
    WRC affiliated with 22
    WTVJ affiliated with 21
NBC Entertainment 2, 87
NBC News 1, 2–3, 23, 38, 57, 59, 84, 94
NBC News at Sunrise (TV program) 36
Newman, David 15
news anchors, television 100–101
news broadcasters
    advancement 105
    books about 109–110
    earnings 105–106
    employers 104
    exploring 103–104
    high school and postsecondary training 102
    job overview 99–102
    organizations and websites about 110–112
    outlook 107
    requirements 102–103
    starting out 104–105
    work environment 106–107
Newsweek 17–18, 30, 71, 75
New York Times 37–38, 42
Noriega, Manuel 26

Norville, Deborah 36, 37, 40
Now with Tom Brokaw and Katie Couric (TV program) 52, 95

O

Oprah Winfrey Show, The (TV program) 64–67

P

Parenting 81
Pauley, Jane 5, 35, 36, *37*, 54
People 54–55
Perot, Ross 63
Powell, Joanna 72
Poznek, Nancy 55
Priceman, Marjorie 81
Primetime (TV program) 54
Procter & Gamble 67
Project for Excellence in Journalism and the Committee of Concerned Journalists 112

R

Radio-Television News Directors Association 105, 112
Radio-Television News Directors Foundation 112
Rather, Dan 1, 75, 88
Reader's Digest 11, 90
Reagan, Ronald 20
Reasoner, Harry 14
Rivera, Geraldo 50, 67
Rivera Live (TV program) 67
Roker, Al 58, 65, 67
Roseanne (TV program) 80
Rowling, J. K. *86*
Russert, Tim 25

S

Saturday Nightly News (TV program) 26
Savitch, Jessica 5
Sawyer, Diane 1, 5, 54, 75
Schneider, Karen 54–55
Schonfeld, Reese 17, 20
Schwarzkopf, H. Norman 31
Scott, Willard 35, 48, 51, 65
Senate, U.S. 77
Shapiro, Neal 2
Shark Tale (animated film) 90, 97
Simmons, Sue 4
Simpson, Nicole Brown 57
Simpson, O. J. 57, 58–59, 68, 90, 96
60 Minutes (TV program) 52, 54, 85
Smart, Elizabeth 88
Spielberg, Steven 84–85
sports anchors 100–101
Stahl, Leslie 5, 54

T

Take Two (TV program) 18–20, 93
Tales from the Bed: On Living, Dying and Having It All (Estess) 83, 97
talk shows 114
Tartikoff, Brandon 72, 88
Tartikoff, Lilly 72–73
terrorist attacks of 9/11 84, 96
3rd Rock from the Sun (TV program) 80
Time 30, 41, 79, 85
"*Today* Girl" 34

Today (TV program)
   Brokaw on 35, 39, 58
   Chancellor on 34
   Couric on 1–4, 30–31, 36–44, *37*, 46–52, 53–54, 55–56, 57–59, 61–64, 65, *66*, *66*, 67, 69, 70–71, 72, 75–77, 79, 83–91, *89*, 94–97
   Downs on 34–35
   Garroway on 34
   Gumbel on 35–36, 37, 38, *39*, 40, 41, 48, 51, 55, 57, 58, 59, 63, 64, 65, 94
   history of 33–38
   Lauer on 1, 58, 59, 64–67, *66*, 69, 70–71, 77, 85, 95
   Muggs on 34
   Norville on 36–37
   Pauley on 35, *37*
   Scott on 35, 48, 51, 65
   Touchet at 87, 97
   Wald at 87
   Wallace on 35
   Walters on 13, 35, *37*
   Zucker at 2, 50, 52, 63, 64, 95
Tonight (TV program) 33
Touchet, Tom 87, 97
Turner, Ted 16
TV Guide 21, 38, 47, 84, 96
20/20 (TV program) 54
2002 Radio and Television Salary Survey 105

U

United Press International 7
University of Maryland 7
University of Virginia 12, 14, 93

W

Wald, Jonathan 87
Walker, Wendy 16, 26
Wallace, Chris 35
Walters, Barbara 1, 5, *13*, 13–14, 35, *37*, 39, 54, 75, 85
Washington and Lee University 27
Washington Post 85
Watson, George 16
Weaver, Sylvester "Pat" 33–34
Weber, Bruce 42
Werner, Tom 80, 96
What Your Doctor May Not Tell You About Colorectal Cancer (Pochapin) 83, 97
Wide, Wide World (TV program) 33
Williams and Connolly 28
Women's Wear Daily 61
World News Tonight (TV program) 15
World Wide Web 101
WRC 22–24, 26, 94
WTVJ 21–22, 94

Y

Yates, Andrea 84
Your Show of Shows (TV program) 33

Z

Zucker, Jeff 2, 50, 52, 63, 64, 68, 76, 87, 95

ABOUT THE AUTHOR

James Robert Parish, a former entertainment reporter, publicist, and book series editor, is the author of numerous biographies and reference books of the entertainment industry including *Stan Lee: Comic-Book Writer*; *Twyla Tharp: Choreographer*; *Denzel Washington: Actor*; *Halle Berry: Actor*; *Stephen King: Writer*; *Tom Hanks: Actor*; *Steven Spielberg: Filmmaker*; *Katharine Hepburn: The Untold Story*; *The Hollywood Book of Scandal*; *Whitney Houston*; *The Hollywood Book of Love*; *Hollywood Divas*; *Hollywood Bad Boys*; *The Encyclopedia of Ethnic Groups in Hollywood*; *Jet Li*; *Gus Van Sant*; *The Hollywood Book of Death*; *Whoopi Goldberg*; *Rosie O'Donnell's Story*; *The Unofficial "Murder, She Wrote" Casebook*; *Today's Black Hollywood*; and *Let's Talk! America's Favorite TV Talk Show Hosts*.

Mr. Parish is a frequent on-camera interviewee on cable and network TV for documentaries on the performing arts both in the United States and in the United Kingdom. Mr. Parish resides in Studio City, California. Mr. Parish's website is http://www.jamesrobertparish.com.

	DATE DUE		

48920

B
COU

Parish, James Robert.

Katie Couric : TV news broadcaster

559462 02496   47242D   002